Ans	_____	M.L.	_____
ASH	_____	MLW	_____
Bev	_____	Mt.Pl	_____
C.C.	_____	NLM	_____
C.P.	_____	Ott	_____
Dick	_____	PC	_____
DRZ	_____	PH	_____
ECH	_____	P.P.	2/08 _____
ECS	_____	Pion.P.	10/09 _____
Gar	_____	Q.A.	_____
GRM	_____	Riv	_____
GSP	_____	RPP	_____
G.V.	_____	Ross	11/08 (Lydies) 2/09
Har	_____	S.C.	_____
JPCP	_____	St.A.	_____
KEN	8/08 _____	St.J	_____
K.L.	7/07 (S2my)	St.Joa	_____
K.M.	_____	St.M.	_____
L.H.	_____	Sgt	_____
LO	_____	T.H.	_____
Lyn	_____	TLLO	_____
L.V.	2/10 _____	T.M.	_____
McC	_____	T.T.	_____
McG	_____	Ven	_____
McQ	_____	Vets	_____
MIL	_____	VP	_____
GRM - 12/09 Hansen		Wat	_____
_____		Wed	_____
_____		WIL	_____
_____		W.L.	_____
_____		_____	
_____		_____	
_____		_____	

PRECIOUS MOMENTS

The heartbreak was all behind her, but hearing her name mentioned on the radio, and that song — their special song — brought bittersweet memories rushing back through the years. It had to be a coincidence, and was best forgotten — but then Lara opened the door to find her past standing there. The moment of truth she had dreaded for years had finally arrived, and she wasn't sure how to handle it . . .

Books by June Gadsby
in the Linford Romance Library:

PRECIOUS LOVE
KISS TODAY GOODBYE
SECRET OBSESSIONS
THE ROSE CAROUSEL
THE SAFE HEART
THE MIRACLE OF LOVE
VALLEY OF DREAMS

JUNE GADSBY

PRECIOUS MOMENTS

Complete and Unabridged

LINFORD
Leicester

First published in Great Britain in 2006

First Linford Edition
published 2007

British Library CIP Data

Gadsby, June
  Precious moments.—Large print ed.—
Linford romance library
  1. Love stories
  2. Large type books
  I. Title
  823.9'2 [F]

ISBN 978–1–84617–718–7

Published by
F. A. Thorpe (Publishing)
Anstey, Leicestershire

Set by Words & Graphics Ltd.
Anstey, Leicestershire
Printed and bound in Great Britain by
T. J. International Ltd., Padstow, Cornwall

This book is printed on acid-free paper

1

'Yeah! Yeah! Wow!' The twins were in the garden making rainbows. They were screaming with excitement as water sprayed everywhere, producing acres of translucent colour as it was touched by the rays of the morning sun. Normally, it did Lara's heart good to hear them sound so happy. But today she was numb, as of ten minutes ago.

The radio had been playing all morning without her paying too much attention. It was good, therapeutic background music when you were preparing a family Sunday lunch.

However, she had been taken completely off-guard by a request that had gone out on the 'Lost Loves' slot.

'So there you are, folks,' the presenter said. 'A real tearjerker for you. Lara, if you're listening and you want to contact Martin, just send us a word. In the meantime, Martin had asked us to play this especially for you.'

The introductory bars of the song filled the kitchen. With her mouth dry and her heart thumping in her chest, Lara switched off the radio and stood there glaring at it, frozen in time. And the twins were watching her, wide-eyed with curiosity.

Before they could start plying her with questions she had ordered them out of the kitchen, more crossly than they deserved, which was probably why they were making more noise than usual.

That request couldn't possibly mean her, she thought desperately. It had to be some other couple with the same names. There were lots of Martins and probably quite a few Laras, too. In fact, she had often wondered if these programmes were fictitious and only scripted to sound real.

She tried to ignore it as the Sunday roast sizzled and the fumes from the onions she was chopping got to her eyes, making them water. She had kept her sights on her two lovely children and tried to block Martin out of her thoughts.

Bad enough that they had played the love song he used to sing to her, without the added coincidence of the names. And did it have to fall on this of all days? The whole business was giving her heart a particularly cruel tweak.

Lara saw the twins glance towards the open kitchen window, their ten-year-old faces suddenly unsmiling and resentful. She thought, for a moment, it was because of her, then saw that her mother had just arrived.

Even as Evelyn was getting out of the car, she could be heard chastising Janie and Tim for making a noise and wasting water. Sunday lunch with their grandmother was always fraught with dark moments. Thank goodness it didn't happen every week, Lara thought.

She turned away, feeling sandwiched between opposing emotions. Her children on the one hand, her mother on the other. It was never easy to strike a happy medium between the two, but Lara was determined to do her best. There was enough weighing on her mind without falling out with Evelyn.

'Gran's arrived.'

Tim's rather peeved voice, stating the obvious, hailed her through the open window and she looked up to see two hot faces, healthy cheeks glistening with hose water, but minus the happy smiles of a few minutes ago.

'She's brought somebody with her,' Janie said.

Janie was the absolute double of her brother, except for her long, silky hair, which had come undone. She blew it out of her eyes and heaved a long, exasperated sigh.

Lara avoided her daughter's probing eyes. 'I told you about it, remember? His name is Desmond Mayhew. He's your gran's solicitor.'

'Why's she bringing her solicitor . . . ?' Tim began, but was nudged into silence by his sister.

The two faces continued to regard Lara, their eyes suspicious and questioning and suddenly she felt she couldn't handle it. Yet another of her mother's matchmaking attempts was about to unroll and spoil her otherwise tranquil life.

'Please, you two,' she pleaded over her shoulder as she basted the roast of lamb in the oven. 'Be good. Go and tidy yourselves up before your gran starts lecturing. You know what she's like.'

There were groans in tandem from the windowsill upon which two sets of elbows were now resting.

'Do we have to?' Tim always felt it necessary to object, though he only ever did it half-heartedly. It was his way of asserting his male superiority over the females in the family.

'You could tell Gran that we've gone to our friends' for lunch,' Janie said, resting her chin on her hands and looking hopeful.

'Yeah!' Tim enthused. 'And you could sneak us some lunch upstairs on plates as if we were fugitives. That'd be really cool, Mum.'

Lara stifled a laugh, thinking that all three of them behaved somewhat like fugitives when Evelyn was around. Her mother had no understanding when it came to her grandchildren. Or her only daughter, if it came to that.

'Go on, off you go or I'll give your meal to Spike.'

Spike was a dog they had inherited with the house. Some kind of undetermined crossbred with immensely long legs, an idiotic face that laughed constantly, and grey fur that stuck out in spikes all over his body. Hence the name. He was old, the house was ancient, and both were in need of a lot of TLC.

It was easy with the dog. They just had to feed him, give him plenty of cuddles and a daily walk. The house was a different matter altogether. Lara did what she could, but even her DIY talents were not enough to save the old place from falling apart at the seams. It needed a man on the job for that and it was the one thing this household lacked.

Lara stared again at the silent radio. Sunday was the only time she made a conscious effort to listen. All those old romantic songs were great to relax to. She just hadn't expected to hear that song, or the reaction it provoked in her. OK, it was an oldie, it was aeons out of date, but still wonderful, still so, so romantic.

When will I see you again — when will we share precious moments . . . ?

As it played round and round in her head a lump came into her throat. She gave herself a mental kick and thought how stupid it all was.

'Coo-ee!'

Lara's mother stomped enthusiastically in the direction of the kitchen, having first deposited her latest candidate for the ever-vacant post of son-in-law in the sitting-room. Hurriedly, Lara brushed a stray tear from her cheek and forced a welcoming smile, noticing that the twins, still grubby and full of curiosity, came too.

'Why are you crying, Mum?' Janie wanted to know, her eyes as big and as round as dinner plates.

'She always cries when she hears that song,' Tim announced.

'Which song is that?' Evelyn looked from one to the other expectantly.

'It's just a soppy love song,' Tim informed her with a wry grin.

At which point, Janie decided to give her version of the song in question, warbling at the top of her voice and ignoring her mother's pleas to 'stop at once'.

'That's quite enough, dear!' Evelyn said sharply. 'I don't think we need to hear more, thank you very much.'

'Please go and get washed, children,' Lara said, feeling her jaw set tightly, remembering her own strict upbringing when there was never any allowance for free expression of any kind.

'We're early,' Evelyn said, 'You don't mind, do you?'

Lara did mind, but she would never have said so. When her mother came to lunch she automatically got through the day just below the stressed out limit. When it consisted of mother plus possible-husband to-be-for-only-daughter-who-was-deserted-by-husband-after-only-three-months-of-marriage, it was ten times more difficult.

And now there was that silly love song that brought back so many memories of being in love for the first and only time. She had foolishly believed that Martin would be there in her world forever.

Lara felt the tension in her heart spread throughout her body and her eyelids prickled with fresh tears.

'Mum's crying again,' Tim said, not helping matters at all.

It gave Evelyn a reason to fix her daughter with an all-embracing regard.

'What on earth happened?' she asked in her strident voice. 'Have you had bad news?'

'No, of course not, Mum,' Lara said

quickly, chopping onions at a frantic rate. 'Onions always make me cry.'

'Come and meet Desmond.'

'I can't, Mum. Not right now. The lunch will spoil.'

Evelyn stared at her daughter and that all-knowing look of the armchair oracle came into her expression.

'Is it something to do with that boy you married?' Evelyn asked.

She had never liked Martin. Evelyn had stiffened her spine and her expression, at Lara's announcement that she and Martin were going to get married. At seventeen and nineteen respectively, neither of them really knew what they were doing. Lara knew that now, but they had been so desperately in love at the time.

She could remember her mother shrieking at her. 'How can you put me through this, Lara? You're pregnant, of course! How could you! My life is ruined.'

Lara had not been pregnant, but there was no arguing with Evelyn when she had a bee in her maternal bonnet.

The twins were still hovering, silent and grubby, but at least they knew how to behave in the presence of their authoritarian grandmother, even if it did take a lot of self-control. This required them to be mature and wise beyond their years. Lara thought they did very well, in the circumstances. She couldn't help but be proud of them.

Tim, who was by far the most sensitive of the two children, suddenly launched himself at Lara and gave her a great bear-hug. Janie followed with a self-conscious kiss on the cheek, and whispered: 'Don't be sad, Mum, please!'

'Sad? What have you got to be sad about?' Evelyn looked from one to the other for explanation and they blinked silently back at her. 'Well?'

'Nothing, Mum,' she said, ushering them all out of the kitchen. 'Nothing at all.'

'Hmm,' Evelyn said doubtfully and gave her daughter a searching look before leading the way back into the living-room, where Desmond Mayhew, looking decidedly uncomfortable, was waiting.

'Hello,' their guest said, a little uncertainly and gripped the hand Lara held out to him. 'It's very kind of you to invite me.'

'Not at all — a pleasure!' Lara spoke a little too brightly, wishing he wouldn't look at her quite so intently. 'Mum has told me all about you.'

'How boring for you,' he said with a smile that wasn't at all unpleasant. 'I can't imagine what you would find of interest in the life of your mother's solicitor. She probably embroidered on it a little.'

'Lara, dear,' Evelyn said, taking her daughter to one side and looking every inch the concerned mother. 'Do go and fix your make-up. You have mascara all over your face.'

Embarrassed, Lara rushed to the bathroom, cursing herself for being so instantly obedient, like the good, brainwashed daughter she had always been. However, when she observed herself in the bathroom mirror she was appalled at the damage that that one love song had wrought.

It was a wonder Desmond hadn't fallen about laughing, so that was at least a point in his favour.

When she returned to the sitting-room, it was to find Tim and Janie more than capably in charge of the pre-luncheon drinks. Her mother, as usual, was nursing a rather large sweet sherry and Janie was in process of giving the accountant a gigantic gin and tonic. Lara preyed fervently that it was mostly made up of tonic, but she doubted it somehow.

The twins finally disappeared, giggling excitedly and muttering to one another all the way up the stairs. Lara, clutching a small glass of dry white wine, sat as far from their guest as she could manage, but too close to her mother for comfort.

'That's better, Lara,' Evelyn said,

inspecting her daughter's newly-scrubbed and refurbished face. 'So — what were you crying about, hmm?'

Her mother, always the queen of the unfortunate remark, was waiting for a response to her embarrassing question.

Lara shook her head and drank deeply, almost emptying her glass and feeling the rush of unaccustomed alcohol to her head.

'Don't be silly, Mum,' she said, giving a hasty glance in Desmond's direction; he was tactfully pretending not to notice the exchange between mother and daughter. 'It was just the onions, as I told you.'

'Timmy said that it all started when you were listening to something on the radio and that you always cried when you heard that same old love song. His words, not mine. That child is far too sensitive for his own good. He needs a man's influence.'

Lara shifted in her seat uncomfortably as her mother shot a pointed glance across the room. She got up and refilled her glass, which was better than staying where she was and having those beady little hawk-like eyes cutting through to her soul.

'He's a romantic at heart, just like me,' she said, her back to the room and her mother in particular. 'It's not a crime.'

There was a short, electric silence, after which everyone started speaking together. They laughed nervously, then a further silence took over and Lara felt like an unwelcome guest in her own sitting-room.

The twins reappeared, washed and tidy, saving the situation. However, after a few minutes of dutiful rapport with their grandmother, they turned their attention to Desmond and put him through some third-degree questioning, which he didn't seem to mind at all.

'You're not going to marry him, are you?' Janie whispered in Lara's ear as they dished out the pudding two hours later. 'He's not exactly awesome, is he?'

'That's very unkind, Janie,' Lara

muttered with a glance all round to make sure nobody else had heard her daughter's words. 'Now, take this dish to Gran, then you and Tim can be excused.'

Janie and Tim grinned with relief and nodded. There was great complicity between Lara and her children. She often found them easier to communicate with, despite their tender years, than many an adult.

'It's very difficult, trying to raise children without a partner,' Desmond said as he eventually said goodbye.

'It has its moments,' she told him. 'Most of them good, quite frankly.'

Evelyn, of course, found a reason to double back, leaving Desmond sitting in her car.

'What on earth is wrong with you, girl?' Evelyn demanded, obviously put out by her daughter's behaviour, though Lara thought she had coped admirably, everything considered.

'I bring you a very desirable marriage prospect and you treat him like . . . '

'Don't, Mum,' Lara stopped her mother in mid-sentence, which earned her a harsh look. 'As I keep telling you, I'm perfectly happy without a man in my life. Desmond seems very nice, but you can forget your idea of him as my new partner. Even if I were looking for someone new, which I'm not, there would have to be a spark and there wasn't.'

Evelyn's sigh was of mammoth proportions. 'Darling Lara, you don't know what a proper partner is like. I ask you, look at the last one — that so-called husband of yours. He got you pregnant and couldn't wait to run off, leaving you with your hands full.'

'Oh, Mum!'

With a haughty expression, Evelyn marched back down the garden path to the car. No doubt, by the time she took Desmond home, he would be in full knowledge of Lara's miserable past, deftly embroidered upon by Evelyn.

2

'It is, I tell you! It's got to be him!' Tim said decisively, while staring resolutely at his twin sister.

'Be quiet, Tim. She'll hear you.'

Tim's voice was raised in excitement and Janie's could be heard barely half an octave lower. Lara hesitated, half way up the stairs, wondering what her two children were getting up to. They appeared to be in her bedroom, which was surprising, because they didn't normally go in there. Bedrooms were private domains and Tim and Janie were good at respecting house rules.

'She can hear you and she's coming right now,' Lara called out.

After suppressed gasps, there followed a moment's shocked silence, then some scuffling and the twins got rid of the evidence of their mischief, whatever that might be.

'Sorry, Mum!' they said in unison as Lara regarded them from the open doorway.

There wasn't any damage, so they hadn't broken anything; no stains, so nothing had been spilled. The bed cover was slightly rumpled and a drawer had not been properly closed. Lara gave them her best maternal frown and waited for an explanation. She didn't have to tell them that she was well displeased.

'We were only . . . ' Tim began and stopped at a sharp look from his sister, arresting the too-ready flow of words.

' . . . chasing a butterfly!' Janie finished for him, looking pleased with herself, though Tim's obvious guilt told Lara that there was something more afoot than a butterfly chase.

'I hope you let it escape,' she said, testing the waters.

'Mm-mm!' Janie nodded vigorously and as she did, something dropped out of the hand she was holding behind her back, something big and heavy.

Janie's eyes rose to the ceiling and Tim groaned, his face twisting into an expression of disbelief.

'What's that you were hiding?' Lara demanded, stepping forward and seeing the familiar leather-bound volume lying haphazardly on the carpet, its pages dislodged.

She bent to retrieve the precious photograph album, trying not to be too angry when she saw how one page had received a bent corner in the fall. Sitting on the bed, she put the album on her lap and smoothed out the page, her throat tightening as her fingers touched the wedding photograph.

There she was, eleven years younger, quite pretty, extraordinarily happy and totally naïve. And Martin was beside her, the proud groom. How boyish he looked, how proud, grinning from ear to ear.

'We didn't mean to damage it, Mum,' Janie said. 'We just wanted to look at the photographs.'

Lara remembered now that they had

seen her poring over the pages last night and she had hurriedly put it away out of sight. She hadn't looked at those photographs in years. After Martin left, she had been tempted to burn them, as her mother had instructed her to do.

She couldn't do it. Of course not. Those images represented too much happiness in her past. No matter what had happened afterwards, nothing could wipe out the good times already experienced.

'Is that our father?' Tim asked, suddenly looking close to tears himself and she prayed that he would not cry. How could she hold on to her own dignity if her ten-year-old son cried over his missing father? Someone he had never known.

'Yes,' she said and had to clear her throat a couple of times, before she could go on. 'That's us on our wedding day.'

'You look happy,' Janie said, sitting down beside her and pushing up close.

'We were happy, Janie.'

She had never told the children what really happened, only that Martin had gone away before they were born and never came back. Her mother wanted her to tell them that Martin was dead, but Lara didn't think that any mother should lie to her children.

'Do you still love him?' Tim's sensitivity was showing.

Lara's breathing was becoming difficult as though something heavy were sitting on her chest. She had always avoided questions of this sort, but her children were now of an age to be more curious and wouldn't easily be put off.

'I don't know,' she said, as honestly as she could. 'I don't think so.'

'Oh, but he looks so nice,' Janie said, gently touching the photograph face of her father staring up at her from the album's stiff page.

'He was nice,' Lara heard her voice start to fracture. 'But he left us and . . . well, it was a long time ago . . . '

'Did you get a divorce?'

Amazingly, it was the first time the

subject had been broached. She shook her head. How many times had she thought about divorce? Too many. And she had never been able to go through with it. This was not helped by the fact that she had no idea where Martin was.

She had tried to contact him over and over again, without success. His parents lived in France and had not even come back for their son's wedding. She had never met them.

Day after day, Lara had waited to hear from Martin, but to no avail. It was as if he had disappeared from the face of the earth. If it had not been for the note he had left her, she might have thought him dead somewhere.

Dear Lara, I know this is unforgivable of me, but I don't think I was cut out for marriage. I'm so sorry to hurt you like this, but I'm taking myself out of your life. Don't spend too much time missing me. I'm not worth it. All my love, forever, Martin.

His silence had lasted more than a decade, until this morning. If it was, indeed, her Martin who was mentioned on the radio, and she doubted that very much.

All my love, forever! How could he love her and still walk out on her, knowing that she was pregnant?

'Let's go out for a walk, shall we?' Lara slid the album away in her drawer. 'Come on. Spike needs some exercise and so do I.'

Her suggestion was met with an uneasy silence.

'I still have some homework to do, Mum,' Janie said with a quick glance at her brother.

Tim nodded vigorously. 'Me too.'

She tried to persuade them, but in the end, it was the twins who persuaded her to go out alone with Spike for half-an-hour. It wasn't something she usually did, leave them on their own in the house. However, they were sensible for their age and she really did need to get away for a short while and breathe some fresh air. Just a few minutes would help.

'Here, Spike!' she called and the dog came running, long pink tongue lolling, his shaggy face lighting up with canine excitement at the prospect of a walk.

★   ★   ★

A couple of weeks had passed since the Sunday lunch with her mother, so Lara was surprised to pick up the phone one evening and find Desmond at the other end.

'I hope I'm not ringing too late,' he said.

Lara assured him that she never went to bed early at the weekends because she didn't have to get up for work the next day. She worked at home, providing a typing and proofreading service, but she tried to stick to office hours.

It didn't pay much, but it was very much a case of being grateful for what she could get, since she was unqualified, having married so young. Only this year had she been able to afford an Open University Course in Business

Studies and she was enjoying the challenge.

'I wondered if you would like to go out for a drink sometime?'

Lara blinked at the telephone receiver in her hand. This was a bit unprecedented. She really hadn't expected to see Desmond Mayhew again. Nor had she really wanted to, but it would be so nice to go out on a date once in a while. It didn't have to lead to anything serious.

'It'll have to be a time when I can get a babysitter,' she said.

'Don't worry about that,' he said. 'I have two of my own. They stay with me during the school holidays and most weekends. We could all go somewhere together tomorrow afternoon, if you've nothing on.'

'Oh!' Lara was taken by surprise. She hadn't known anything about his private life, except that he was single. 'You're divorced then?'

'Two years ago. It was quite amicable, thank heavens.'

'Well, I'm not sure . . . '

'It's all right, Lara. Your mother told me about your situation. If you really don't want to come I'll understand.'

Lara chewed on her mouth as she reflected. He seemed a nice enough man, so why not go out with him. It wasn't as if he had demanded a commitment of any kind, was it?

'Yes, all right. It sounds quite a good idea. Let's pray for sunshine,' she said with a laugh, looking through the window at the rain coming down in torrents.

'I'll pick you up at midday and we can take the kids out for lunch. Their choice of venue. I hope you like hamburger and chips.'

Lara groaned and gave another laugh. He joined in and suddenly he wasn't a stranger any more.

'See you tomorrow, then,' he said.

She put the phone down and stared at it a long time, feeling a sudden rise of butterflies in her stomach. It was like being a young girl again, about to go out on a date with a new man. It was also a little scary. She hadn't been out on a date in a very long while.

* * *

When the next day dawned the sun struggled valiantly through a milky mist and it looked all set for a pleasant afternoon. Lara pottered about the house, unable to settle. It was stupid, but she was far more nervous than she expected to be. The twins, however, were blasé about the whole thing.

'Why does he want us to go with you?' Tim wanted to know.

'Because he'll have his children with him,' Lara told him and saw Janie pull a wry face. 'Now don't go all babyish on me and make me ashamed. I'm sure you'll enjoy it, really.'

Her mother phoned just before Desmond was due. She had heard the news that Lara and Desmond were going out together and was already hearing wedding bells. Lara, however, put her right on that.

'It's just an outing between friends, Mum,' she said. 'Nothing romantic, so don't start imagining things.'

Evelyn wittered on for a few minutes more, then Lara had to excuse herself to go and get ready. She was just putting the final touches to her face when the doorbell rang out and her heart lurched.

She sat there, feeling uncomfortable and wishing she hadn't agreed on this outing after all. Suppose he did have designs on her, as her mother suspected?

'There's someone at the door, Mum,' Janie came into her room and told her as if she must be deaf.

'Yes, I know, love.' Lara's smile wavered slightly. 'It'll be Desmond and his children. Would you go and let them in. I'll be there in a moment.'

Janie didn't move. As she stood there, stork-like, rubbing one foot up and down the back of her other leg, her brother came to join her.

'There's somebody at the door, Mum,' he repeated, parrot-fashion.

'Yes, I know! It's Desmond. What on earth is wrong with you two? Go and let the poor man in.'

'It's not Desmond,' they said in unison with an exchange of nervous glances as the doorbell rang a second time.

Lara frowned and sighed. They were up to something, she could tell. In fact, they had been acting strangely for some time, but questioning had simply resulted in shrugged shoulders and expressions of false innocence. They were growing up too fast and she wasn't sure that she liked it.

Blotting her lipstick and checking her appearance in the long cheval mirror, Lara hurried down the stairs, the children following close at her heels. They bumped into her in the hall when she hesitated before opening the front door.

'Look out!' she gasped and pulled the door wide, surprised to find that it was not Desmond on the other side of it. 'Can I help you?'

The words were out before she recognised his face. Then she was swallowing hard, one hand grasping at her throat, the other holding on fast to the door for support.

'Martin?'

He had changed in the eleven years since she had seen him, but then he was no longer a gangling youth with a cheeky grin. He was a mature man of thirty. He wore his hair short, but it was just as dark with only the tiniest fleck of grey at the temples. He had filled out and looked broader, more muscular. He looked — good.

'Hello, Lara,' he said in the same soft, caressing voice she remembered all too well.

'How did you . . . ?' She had to clear her throat and start again. 'How did you know where to find me?'

His forehead creased as if she had asked him a question he didn't understand. Staring at her intently, he rubbed the back of his neck. It was a mannerism she was familiar with. He did it when he was puzzled or bothered by something.

'But you sent me your address.'

'I what?'

Martin looked up and down the street, obviously searching for words, looking for explanations.

'After I — after I sent out that plea on the radio for you to get in touch with me if — if you still cared . . . ' He broke off and she heard his long intake of breath. 'It was you who replied, wasn't it?'

She started to shake her head, then felt the twins pressed up tightly against her. She licked her lips and stepped back, saw his eyes leave her and flicker over the two children he didn't know he had.

'You'd better come in,' she said.

3

'So, it was you who put out that radio message?' Lara felt a sudden urge of heat; her skin prickled.

Martin nodded, his eyes growing large like two dark moons. 'Yes, but I didn't really expect you to reply, even if you heard it, let alone agree to see me.'

'Why did you do it, then? After all this time? I thought — well, I'm not sure what I thought.'

'I can understand how bitter you must have felt. It was a cruel thing for anyone to do — walk away like that. Cruel and cowardly.'

The last thing Lara wanted was to get into an argument over something that was long dead. Best to stay calm and reasonable.

'We were both too young,' she said after a long pause. 'Our parents were right.'

Martin nodded slowly, his eyes fixed on her, those big sherry brown eyes that were tearing at her heart. He seemed incapable of looking away.

'I can't tell you how much I've hated myself,' he said, his voice faltering. 'And yet, you've proved to me that you still care and I can't believe my luck.'

Lara made a couple of false starts, the truth of the situation slowly breaking through her consciousness.

'Martin, I'm sorry to have to say this, but I wasn't the one who replied to your message.'

As she spoke, a movement caught her eye and she turned in time to see the twins backing surreptitiously away out of the room, their faces stricken with guilt.

'Just a minute you two!'

Martin, registering surprise, finally took his eyes from her and stared at the two children. They had come to a halt, wedged shoulder to shoulder in the doorway, two small pillars of salt, identical and indivisible.

'I'm not sure that I understand,' Martin said, his voice almost a whisper.

'Well, you wouldn't, would you?' Lara's anger was rising to counteract the destructive emotions that were warring in her breast. 'The minute you heard that I was pregnant you took off and I never heard from you again. Did you ever wonder whether you had a son or a daughter — or any children at all?'

'Lara, I . . . ' Martin spread his hands and his eyes squeezed tightly shut for a split second. 'I've never stopped thinking about you, but . . . '

'Well, you could have fooled me,' Lara said, thinking that her words sounded so corny.

She reached out and grasped Tim's shoulder, drawing him back into the room and Janie came with him. 'Meet your son. This is Tim.'

Martin's eyes burned into the boy and Tim shrank momentarily before his intense gaze.

'And this is Janie — your daughter. Tim, Janie . . . ' Lara drew a deep breath. 'Children, meet your father.'

Janie flashed a smile while Tim's eyes grew dark and troubled and his chin quivered uncontrollably. As for Martin, he looked like someone awakening from a bad dream.

She could see that all three were filled with suppressed emotion, as was she, but she needed to be strong, needed to bluff it out. For her own sake she needed to be in control of the situation.

Martin shook his head in disbelief, his gaze swivelling from one to the other of the children and back again as he tried to take in the fact that he had not one, but two offspring. Then his gaze came to rest, finally, on Lara and she could see he was lost for words.

'You'd better sit down,' she said. 'Can I offer you a glass of wine? I'm afraid I don't have anything stronger.'

He took a long time to reply and she wondered if he had even heard her. When he finally spoke, his voice was husky, not much more than a whisper.

'A cup of coffee would be welcome, if it's not too much trouble,' he said and she nodded and headed for the kitchen.

Once alone, Lara felt her body give way to trembling. Her legs were turning to jelly. She clutched at the bench for support and took some deep breaths.

Outside, there was the crunch of car wheels on gravel and she guessed that Desmond had arrived for their first outing together. How was she going to explain Martin's presence to him? She couldn't even explain it to herself.

'Tim, Janie!' she called out, aware that her voice sounded strangely foreign and shaky. 'That sounds like Desmond arriving. Can you let him in please?'

At the sound of footsteps and voices in the hall she hurriedly threw coffee into the coffee machine, spilling it all over the bench in her agitated state. She added water, switched on and waited, clinging desperately to the bench until the final hiss subsided into a gentle putter and the coffee was ready. But was she ready to face what was waiting for her in the next room?

With the tray rattling with cups of coffee and soft drinks for the children, she made her way back to the living room, from where she could hear a low mutter of voices and childish laughter that sounded just a little false, but then they were all strangers together for the first time.

'Ah!' Desmond jumped to his feet and took the tray from her, placing it on the coffee table in front of Martin, who remained sitting and still in an apparent state of shock. 'I gather you've had a surprise visit.'

'Yes,' Lara said, forcing a wobbly smile. 'Martin and I — I mean — he was — is . . . '

'Your husband,' Desmond helped out and, although he was smiling brightly, she could see a touch of anxiety in his regard. 'The twins went to great lengths to introduce us.'

'Oh, I see.' Lara glanced across at Janie and Tim who were already chattering away amicably with Desmond's two offspring, a teenage boy and a much younger girl.

'I've obviously come at a bad time,' Martin made to get up, but Desmond placed a hand on his shoulder and, when he sat down again, sat beside him.

'Not at all. You weren't to know that we were going out for the day,' Desmond said with an ease that Lara admired. 'I think, perhaps, I'm the one who should go.'

'No, Desmond!' Lara perched on the arm of a chair because she couldn't relax enough to sit properly. 'At least stay for coffee. It will give the children time to get to know one another — break the ice.'

'There doesn't seem too much ice to break there,' Desmond grinned at the four young people gathered around the table at the window, where the older boy was demonstrating his prowess with the latest pocket computer.

'So, it's the first time they've met?' Martin said, looking pointedly at Lara and she nodded woodenly.

'Good coffee, Lara,' Desmond said, then silence fell like a stone while they all sipped coffee and stared at the floor between them.

★   ★   ★

After what seemed a long time, they began to speak simultaneously. It was embarrassing for all of them and Lara felt that it was her responsibility to sort out the difficulty, one way or another. It was, after all, her home, though it was certainly not her fault that this weird little scenario was taking place.

'More coffee?' she asked, floundering for the right words, but they kept escaping her.

The two men shook their heads, so she started to gather together the cups and glasses, conscious that her hands were still shaking.

'Let me help you,' Desmond said softly, taking the tray from her again and going out of the room with it.

She glanced briefly at Martin, who

stared blankly ahead of him, his cheek muscles working, but still not saying anything. Grabbing up a missed glass from the table where the children were totally occupied, she followed Desmond to the kitchen almost at a run.

'I'm so sorry,' she said as she closed the kitchen door behind her. 'I really had no idea that he was going to turn up like this. We haven't seen one another in more than ten years.'

'Don't worry about it, Lara,' he said, gripping her hand and squeezing it. 'These things happen.'

'Not to me,' she said with a touch of animosity. 'I don't know what possessed him, after all this time. To put out a request out on the radio, of all things. And he thinks I replied to it and sent him my address, which I did not. Really, Desmond, I'm furious about the whole business.'

Desmond did an unexpected thing. He leaned forward and planted a kiss on her forehead, which effectively stopped her flood of angry words.

41

'I think the best thing for me to do is take my kids and leave you to it.'

'Oh, but . . . '

'The poor fellow looks shell-shocked. And I have to admit that I was a little taken aback to find him here, but it's not exactly his fault, is it?'

'I suppose not,' Lara sighed, 'but . . . oh dear, it's certainly ruined our day out. I'm so sorry, Desmond. We were looking forward to it.'

Desmond was gracious to the last, almost as though he were well versed in life's little disappointments. And he did seem genuinely disappointed. She could see it in his eyes and his slightly artificial smile.

'There'll be other days, other occasions, I suppose,' he said, his fingers fleetingly touching her cheek.

For some reason, the gesture made Lara irritable and she wished he would go — wished he had never come. How could she think straight with Martin in the living room like a ghost from the past, and Desmond being nice to her in the kitchen? It was too much to cope with in one morning.

She drew away from him abruptly and he stuck his hands into his trouser pockets and looked uncomfortable.

'Well,' he said on a deep sigh, looking around the small kitchen and avoiding her eyes. 'I won't embarrass you any longer. Perhaps you would like to give me a call sometime when you're free? The offer of a day out still stands.'

'You're very kind,' she told him, wondering how she would have reacted if she were in his shoes. But then, men were masters of the cold veneer when emotions got ruffled.

Desmond's children looked a trifle puzzled by the withdrawal of the promised day's outing. It was obvious that they had bonded well with Janie and Tim. As for the twins, they looked a bit apprehensive once they were left alone with Lara and the man she had introduced as their father.

'Come and sit down,' Lara instructed them and saw that well-known exchange of glances that told her they were guilty of something and she knew what that something was. 'Now, I think some explaining is necessary.'

She gave them her most serious look of reprimand and they knew she meant business. Martin, who had been regarding his hands that hung, clasped, between his knees, glanced up occasionally, looking first at Tim, then at Janie.

It was obvious that although he may have sent out the first message calling for her to get in touch, she could not hold him responsible for orchestrating this extraordinary meeting.

'Are you mad with us, Mum?' Tim asked, sniffing and rubbing his nose vigorously.

'I will be if you don't tell me the truth, young man,' she said. 'And please use your hankie.'

He didn't have a handkerchief, of course, so his sister passed him hers and he grimaced at the pink square of cotton with an embroidered flower, but

44

blew his nose on it anyway.

Janie was watching Martin closely, one heel beating time against the sofa where they sat, a sure sign that she was playing for time, even though she knew a confession was inevitable.

'Are you really, really our father?' she asked and the smile he gave her was filled with mixed emotions.

Lara heard him swallow before he replied, saw his eyes grow hard and shiny, then fill with moisture, which he blinked away rapidly.

'Yes, I think I must be,' he said uncertainly and Janie's eyes widened.

'Aren't you sure?'

'No — ah, yes, of course I'm sure.' He spread his hands, stared at them, then looked plaintively at Lara. 'If your mum says I am, then that's how it is.'

'Mum never tells lies,' Tim said sullenly and looked up from beneath lowered brows.

'No,' said Martin. 'She never ever told lies. That was one of the things I liked about her.'

'Do you tell lies?' Janie asked, always the one to bring forth the difficult questions.

'I try not to, but I'm not such a good person as your mother.'

Now, he was smiling at Lara and it was the old Martin she was seeing. Martin with the bright, honest eyes and the smile to die for. Martin who had made her so happy, made her whole. It was suddenly as if they had been transported back in time and she was young again and impossibly in love with the boy everybody liked and predicted would go places.

Where had he gone, she wondered, after he had walked out on her, having heard that she was pregnant? Had he achieved all the things that were expected of him? Oh, there were so many questions, and yet a part of her felt she should tell him to leave right now and never return, ever again.

4

'How many times,' Lara demanded, feeling self-conscious in front of her estranged husband's eyes, 'have I told you not to use my computer unless I'm there to supervise you?'

There was a mumbled apology from each of her children. 'We only wanted to do something nice for you, Mum,' Janie said, nibbling at a ragged cuticle.

'We know you're lonely and . . . ' Tim shot a furtive glance at Martin. 'And you cry every time that soppy love song comes on. You cried even more when you heard that request asking where you were and stuff.'

'And you cry every time you look at — at Dad's photo. You know you do.'

Janie had gone scarlet as she stumbled over the word 'Dad'. How strange and foreign it must seem to them both, Lara thought, to have this stranger sitting a few feet away from them, never having met him, yet knowing he was their father.

'Besides,' Tim added, 'we wanted to know him. You can't not know your own father — no matter how it is.'

Lara and Martin exchanged glances. Lara bit down hard on her lip and struggled to keep a calm exterior, though inside her was a morass of mixed emotions.

'And what do you think of him so far?' Martin asked, leaning forward slightly, apparently coming out of his traumatised state.

Both children grinned shyly. 'He's all right, I suppose,' Tim said, suddenly full of uncertainty.

'I think you look nice,' Janie said. 'Doesn't he, Mum? In fact, I think he looks better than that old photograph you keep drooling over.'

Lara couldn't speak. Her mind was blocked, her mouth clamped tightly shut to stop her lips from quivering.

'Does she really look at my photograph?' Martin asked, sitting up straighter.

His eyes were on her, but she was pretending to busy herself with tidying a variety of items around the room that had no need of her attention, but her hands needed to be occupied.

'All the time!'

Tim was losing his shyness fast, which was unusual for him. That was always a good sign, when meeting new people. Lara wasn't sure that she wanted to see this good sign with Martin.

'I think, children, you should go to your room and . . .'

There was a three-way disagreement and Lara felt a twinge of resentment. How could Martin walk back into their lives like this and ingratiate himself on the twins, taking their side against her?

'Well, all right,' she consented grudgingly. 'But I don't suppose your father will be staying much longer. Will you, Martin?'

Three pairs of eyes regarded her sharply as if she had stung them with a chastising slap.

'Is it true, Lara?' Martin asked. 'Do you look at my photograph?'

'Oh, you know . . . ' Lara searched for the right thing to say. 'It's in my old family album. I often flicked through the pages.'

'I thought you would have thrown it away by now.'

'I should have, but I simply forgot it was there. It was a long time ago.'

'She looks at it all the time,' Janie said, confirming her brother's earlier statement.

'Would you like to see it?' Tim was up off his seat and charging towards the door.

'Tim! Don't you dare — will you come back this minute.'

But Tim was not in a mood to listen to his mother. Not when he had the attention of the father who had been absent from his short life since before he was born.

'Don't be too hard on them, Lara,' Martin said as Janie threw herself down on the sofa next to him.

Lara threw up her hands and cast her gaze to the ceiling. She still felt uncomfortable with the situation. Her heart was beating far too fast and she felt weak and dazed. Before her legs could give way she, too, sat down heavily and clasped her hands together in her lap.

'You have to admit, Martin, that it's something of a novelty for them,' she said. 'You know — to meet your father for the first time at the age of ten.'

'They seem wise and mature beyond their years,' he replied. 'You've done a great job raising them, Lara.'

'Thank you,' she said dryly, inspecting her fingers one by one, the silence between them ringing in her ears.

'I've been assuming that you did it all alone,' he said, again leaning forward. 'But perhaps you've had help — another partner?'

He was fishing for information on her private life and she was tempted to lie to him, tell him that she had someone else. Desmond would have fitted the bill perfectly, but Martin already knew that their relationship, what little there existed, was at a very early stage.

But she had never lied to him and had no intention of doing so now. What would be the point? To make him jealous or unhappy? His eyes already held a wealth of suffering in their dark and moody depths.

'My mother has helped when I needed her — when the children were younger. And Betty, our neighbour, baby-sits occasionally. Fortunately, I work from home — a typing service . . . '

She stopped, feeling she was revealing too much of her life. What difference could it make, Martin knowing anything at all about the wife he deserted a decade ago?

'I paid maintenance — as much as I could manage, but all I had was your mother's address. You did get the money, didn't you . . . ?'

'Of course I did. I put it in a trust fund for the twins to pay for their eventual university fees.' Lara sighed. 'I didn't want money from you, Martin.'

'You must be very proud of yourself,' he said with a sudden flash of the old brilliant smile that she had adored. 'And how is your mother?'

Martin and Evelyn had never got along too wonderfully. Martin had tried hard, Lara would give him that, but he had never come up to the standard that her mother would have wanted for her only daughter.

'She's still the same as ever.'

'Still treats you like a little girl?'

Lara drew in breath and nodded. 'She tries, but she doesn't get away with it these days. I finally grew up, you see.'

He laughed at that. It was more of a soft chuckle, actually, but oh, what a wonderful sound. Lara's heart did a little treacherous leap of joyous nostalgia as the years raced back and she remembered their first, magical meeting. He had dragged her out of the sea after she got out of her depth. It had been summer and the beach was crowded, but there might only have been the two of them.

Lara could almost feel the sand beneath her again, smell the sea, hear the raucous cries of the seagulls wheeling above them as they had that day.

'What about your father?'

She felt a frown crease her forehead and a pain start up behind her eyes as his voice dragged her back to the present.

'He died four years ago — cancer.'

'Oh, God, Lara. I didn't know.'

He looked genuinely sorry. Martin had liked Harry, though her father had been a bit brutal with him to begin with. Harry was the type of man that never pulled his punches, but he had a heart of gold and everybody liked and respected him for his forthright honesty.

'You weren't to know,' Lara said, the resentful side of her silently adding: 'How could you when you went off without leaving a forwarding address.'

'Why didn't you divorce me, Lara?'

She stared at him, finding it difficult to believe that he could bring himself to ask such a question.

'I might have done,' she told him grittily, her hands bunching into tight little fists to stop them from shaking. 'The trouble was, I didn't know where you had gone. I tried to find you for a very long time, then I gave up.'

'But I did send you a letter,' he said haltingly and she saw a shadow of doubt creep over his countenance. 'It was a couple of days after I walked out — just before I joined my parents in France.'

'A letter? I got no letter, Martin.' Was he lying to save his face; she thought not, somehow.

'I sent more than one — first to the little terrace house where we lived, then to your mother's address . . . '

Lara blanched. Another memory came flooding back. Her mother arriving at their cramped, rented accommodation, coming to comfort her distraught daughter. Evelyn picking up mail that had been lying behind the front door, tutting over it, complaining about the amount of junk mail people were sending out these days.

Forty-eight hours later, Lara moved back into her parents' home. It hadn't taken Evelyn long to persuade her young, pregnant, abandoned daughter that it was the best thing to do in the circumstances.

Looking back, Lara remembered how her mother had seemed cagey when letters arrived, secretive almost. It had never occurred to Lara that house bills might actually have been letters for her.

'Oh, lord, Martin.' Lara felt a cold shudder take hold of her. 'She must have destroyed them — my mother. All the time, she kept telling me that you weren't worth thinking about, that I should simply get on with my life, that she would be there to look after me — and our baby . . . '

'Which turned out to be two babies,' Martin gave her a lop-sided grin, but his eyes were sad and introspective. 'That must have given Evelyn something to think about.'

Lara nodded. She hadn't stayed with her parents for more than a few months, then she managed to get a council flat. And her father had bought her a computer, had helped her in so many ways towards becoming independent. It was ironic that he died before she could show him the resilient stuff she was made of and before she could thank him for his support.

She looked at Martin and saw that he was watching her closely and the twins were watching him with open admiration and blatant curiosity.

'Are your parents still alive?' she asked, for they had been considerably older than Evelyn and Harry.

'Yes, but they're thinking of moving back to the UK soon. Something about seeing their grandchildren grow up.'

'Oh, but they don't know . . . '

'About Tim and Janie? No, of course not. But my brother has four kids and my sister three.'

'I see.' Lara felt a tinge of jealousy that she quickly nipped in the bud. 'Have you been living in France all this time?'

'Yes.'

'Have you got another wife?' Janie interrupted suddenly and Lara felt a sinking in her stomach, as she waited for his answer.

'No, Janie,' Martin said. 'Actually, most of the time, there's just me, lots of ducks and chickens, a few pigs and goats . . . '

'Wow!' Tim enthused. 'Are you a farmer, then?'

'Sort of, but it's much more than that.'

Martin went on to explain that he was actually running a self-sufficiency co-operative with his neighbours, who all shared in the profits accrued by the sale of their own wine, cheese and a variety of other exploits. Living in a picturesque village, he explained, had its advantages.

'It's all a bit touristy, I'm afraid, but we make a decent living. I lead pony treks through the Pyrénées a lot of the time. It's hard work, but fun.'

That got a 'Wow!' from the children. Their faces lit up and Lara knew exactly what to expect from them. They did not let her down.

'Oh, Mum, can we go to France?' Janie's fists were pushed up under her chin. Her dream was to own a pony but there had never been enough money even to give her riding lessons.

'If we went to France,' Tim added, 'I could have a pet goat. They're much more interesting than dogs.'

'Except when they butt you in the behind.' Martin smiled and turned to Lara. 'It looks like I've started something here.'

She couldn't bring herself to smile back. There were too many opposing emotions warring inside her heart. How dare he come here today, unannounced, and dangle juicy carrots in front of her children's noses? It was unforgivable.

Even if he had written letters that she hadn't seen because her mother was so set on them not getting back together again.

'I wish you hadn't . . . ' she faltered. 'Actually, Martin, I wish you hadn't come. We were all right — you know. I was managing fine . . . '

'Couldn't we just talk about it?'

'No,' she said as quickly as she could before she could waver. 'No. Just leave an address where you can be contacted. I'll go and see a solicitor and we can draw a line across the past once and for all.'

There were horrified cries from Tim and Janie, but she knew she was right. She had been wrong to hold on to the dream that was Martin. So terribly wrong. Maybe now she would be able to find someone else, get a new life. It just took a quick phone call to a solicitor and a little patience, then it would all be over. It was always best to make a clean break. Wasn't it?

5

When Lara closed the door behind Martin, she didn't know how she felt. Her nerves were all twitchy as if she was filled with too much electricity. Her heart didn't seem to be beating at all, but lay heavily in her chest like a stone. And there was another heavy stone in the pit of her stomach that kept turning over and over.

Something made her open the door again. She half hoped to see Martin standing there, having come back on some pretext or other. Perhaps she even intended to call him back. At least it would give her the opportunity to hold on to him just that little bit longer.

But the street was empty. Only the brake lights of his car were visible, briefly, before he turned into the main road at the end. She went back into the living-room, switched on the television and watched blindly the flashing images of a war zone and atrocities and bereaved relatives crying unashamedly into the camera. She wished she could cry, get the past hour out of her system, but she felt drained of all emotion.

Right down inside her, there was a hurt that was too profound to shed tears over. Now, she was going to have to rebuild the protective walls of her little world. Martin's appearance, out of the blue like that, had torn them down as effectively as a demolition squad attacking a pack of cards.

If only he hadn't put that message out on the radio, she thought, miserably. If only she hadn't heard it, or the twins responded to it on her behalf. If only . . .

'Oh, Mum!' Janie threw herself into her mother's arms and sobbed against her shoulder. 'Why did you send him away? He's our dad and he was so nice. Why do you hate him?'

'Janie, sweetheart — I don't hate him . . . it's just . . . ' Lara's heart was being squeezed, wrung out like a chamois leather. 'You're far too young to understand, but you will, one day, I promise you.'

'I hate him! I'm glad he's gone!'

Tim's voice rang out. He rushed by Lara and Janie, almost knocking over a small table in his haste. Lara reached out, tried to grab his arm, but he shook her off vigorously, his face red and tear-stained.

'Tim, come back. Let me at least try to explain . . . '

But Tim was running clumsily up the stairs. She started to follow him, hearing his sobs erupt, seeing his anguished face briefly as he gained the landing at the top.

'And I hate you too!' he yelled over his shoulder.

Lara, shocked by his outburst, released her daughter and stood up, rocking shakily on legs that no longer seemed to belong to her. Janie sucked in a deep breath, then started up the stairs after her brother, quietly, sedately, without any show of theatrical behaviour.

'It's all right, Janie,' Lara said, woodenly, wishing he had handled the situation better. 'Tim doesn't mean it. He's too soft-hearted to hate anybody, thank goodness.'

'I know he doesn't mean it, Mum,' Janie said from the top of the stairs. 'But he's upset and so am I.'

'Oh, sweetheart, I'm sorry. Come on, let's make a chocolate cake to cheer ourselves up.'

Lara was trying to make light of the situation, but then she saw the genuine distress marking her daughter's face.

'You shouldn't have sent him away, Mum,' Janie whispered, her voice breaking. 'I thought you loved him.'

'Love dies, Janie,' Lara said, feeling her throat constrict, yet there were still no tears in her asking to be shed. 'When you're older you'll . . . '

'Stop saying that! When I'm older. You're always saying it to me and to Tim. I never want to get older if it makes people so unhappy.'

When Laura went to visit her mother, she found Evelyn looking decidedly grey-faced. There was an underlying anger in her narrowed eyes and tight little smile as she greeted her daughter.

'I suppose you've come about Martin,' Evelyn said, even before Lara's foot was over the threshold. 'Oh, yes, you can look at me like that, but how do you think I felt, having him turn up here after all this time, accusing me of . . . Well, never mind that. Are the pair of you getting together again? Is that what this visit is about?'

Lara blinked and shook her head at her mother. Evelyn was always way ahead of events. She would have made a good writer, Lara often thought, the way she concocted stories in her head and embroidered on any snippet of gossip that came her way.

'I didn't send him round to see you, Mum,' she said. 'He did that on his own.'

She sat down in her mother's sitting-room, on the same sofa she and Martin had done their courting. The same pendulum clock made its tick-tock sound as it looked down solemnly at her from the mantelpiece. The same disapproving bronze bust of Beethoven frowned at her.

Her mother's house was an old-fashioned one. It hadn't changed in colour or style since Lara was a small child. Every year the walls were painted a startling white, the doors and windows a creamy magnolia. There were lacy drapes and pink chintzy covers and deep white lamb's wool rugs on a thick pile red carpet. Not even an ornament had changed, everything occupied the same spot, placed just so.

'Well?' Evelyn brought in a tea tray laden with crustless sandwiches and scones and walnut cake oozing with butter icing.

As quickly and as succinctly as she could, Lara related the story of the radio request and the twins' involvement in bringing Martin from France to see her, thinking that she still cared for him.

'After all these years, you would be mad to even contemplate taking him back.' Evelyn glowered at her over the golden rim of her porcelain teacup. 'And he had the gall to put out a message on the radio, naming you. Dear me, how embarrassing. Do you have any idea how many people who know us will have heard it and will now be laughing behind their hands. What a terrible business.'

Lara wanted to tell her mother that she didn't give a hoot what people thought. She knew a fair number who would think the whole thing totally romantic. Had it happened to one of her friends, she would have been ecstatic for them.

'Mum,' she said, deciding to ignore her mother's last statement and plunge right in with the question that was burning holes in her brain. 'Martin says he wrote to me several times. He said he addressed his letters here after I didn't reply to the first one, assuming I had moved in with you, which I had.'

'Well, dear, if you want to believe that . . . '

'Whatever Martin was, Mum, he was never a liar. It was against all his principles.'

'What are you trying to say, Lara?' Evelyn glanced at her watch as if she was anxious to be somewhere.

'Did you or did you not destroy Martin's letters to me?'

There. The question was out in the open. Lara watched her mother's face closely. Martin might not be a liar, but Evelyn most certainly was when the correct words could get her out of a sticky situation. Her face always gave her away. The narrowed eyes that shot off to the side, the slight twitch of a cheek muscle, the drawing in of her nostrils.

At first, Lara thought her mother was not going to respond to her questioning. Whatever was going through Evelyn's head at that moment was distressing her to the extent that she could not keep her thin shoulders still, or her fingers from plucking at her skirt.

'What I did, Lara, I did for your own good,' she said at last. 'You're my daughter and I love you. I didn't want to see you hurt and I thought — I thought that you would meet someone better and Martin would be forgotten.'

'Oh, Mum! Don't you see that what you did was wrong?'

A thin eyebrow shot up, the cheek twitched again as Evelyn stared towards the window rather than meet Lara's accusing eyes.

'I only did what I thought was best for you at the time,' she said. 'I did what any caring mother would have done.'

Lara managed a twisted smile. 'I'm not sure about that, Mum,' she said. 'You interfered in my life without under-standing the details. Maybe Martin and I would have got back together, made our marriage work. I might have been happy now, instead of constantly wondering what went wrong and being unable to progress in my life.'

'I doubt that very much. What kind of man walks out on his pregnant wife after only a few months of marriage? I'll tell you . . . '

'No! I don't want to hear what you think of Martin. It's not for you to judge. You weren't in love with him. You couldn't even take the trouble to get to know him, could you? He wasn't what you wanted for your only daughter. What you wanted. Did you ever consider what I wanted, Mum? Well, did you?'

★   ★   ★

Lara and her mother had not rowed. That would have served no purpose except to inflame the anger that was already in Lara's heart. Instead, she had simply got up and left Evelyn sitting there, staring at her departing figure.

On her way home Lara stopped off at

the supermarket and bought a few items of food and some treats that she knew would please the twins. The atmosphere between them was still heavy, but at least they were speaking to her again.

As she let herself in the front door, she heard the telephone ringing. For one scary moment she wondered if it might be Martin and hesitated almost too long before picking up the receiver.

'Hello, there! How are you?'

It was Desmond and she was almost relieved to hear his voice, though it had taken some moments to recognise who was at the other end.

'I'm fine,' she told him, grimacing into space because she felt anything but fine. 'Look, Desmond, I meant to give you a call and apologise for the other day.'

'Don't give it a second thought,' he said cheerfully. 'At the risk of being indiscreet, Lara, are you and your husband making a fresh start?'

There was a protracted silence while

she listened to his words echoing in her head and Desmond, thinking the line had gone dead was asking if she were still there.

'Sorry — yes, I'm here and . . . ' She swallowed dryly. 'Martin only stayed an hour, then he left. I imagine he's already back in France by now.'

There was a hint of a pause before he went on speaking with a certain amount of terseness in his voice.

'So, it wasn't the grand reunion, then?'

'No, I don't think you could say that.'

What else could she tell him? He was a comparative stranger in her life. The whole situation must have looked extremely bizarre. She was surprised he had bothered to get back in touch after Sunday.

'I see.'

'Look, I think I owe you an explanation,' she said.

'No — no, not at all. But you do owe me a day out with the kids. How about tomorrow, or do you work on Saturdays?'

He was still interested. Well, that was surprising. She cleared her throat and took time to reply, not wishing to sound too available, trying to feel enthusiastic.

'Let me see — ah, if I stay up till midnight tonight I should finish the typescript I'm working on. But I did promise Tim and Janie that I would take them swimming tomorrow afternoon.'

'In the sea?'

She laughed ' . . . er, no. I'm not a strong swimmer, so it has to be the local pool where there's somebody to save me when I get out of my depth. The kids are already strong swimmers, thank goodness.'

'In that case, let's take all four of them to the beach. I'll wear my life-saving medal, if it will make you feel any better. How about that?'

'I — er . . . '

'Please don't say no, Lara. I'd like the opportunity to get to know you better. If it doesn't work out for either of us, there needn't be a return match.'

'Oh, you are straight up front, aren't you?'

She couldn't help smiling into the receiver, thinking that she was beginning to like this man, despite having him thrust upon her by her mother.

'At my age, Lara, I can't afford to waste time. I wasn't born to be a single parent.

Neither was I, Lara thought, wistfully, but kept the remark to herself. His words pushed her into having second thoughts. He wasn't all that much older than she was — ten years maybe, twelve at the most. That would make him about forty, She hoped he wasn't going to be the type of man who rushed women into an intimate relationship for all the wrong reasons. Lara didn't think she was ready for that. Certainly not on their first date.

Ignoring his remark, she cleared the frog from her throat again and fought back the temptation to turn him down.

'What time shall we meet, then?' she asked.

They arranged a time, Desmond insisting that he would come and pick them up in his Espace where there was plenty of room for all six of them, plus Spike. He really was trying to please her, Lara thought.

Spike had not exactly taken to Desmond, who admitted that he had never been much of a dog lover. They tended to regard one another with barely disguised mistrust.

'Spike,' she spoke to the dog that had stolen her own heart and he gazed up at her with adoring eyes. 'Tomorrow, it's best behaviour time, do you hear.'

6

Lara was up bright and early on Saturday morning, having slept badly. The children were once more quiet and secretive and she worried in case the planned day at the seaside might not be a good idea after all. The last thing she wanted was her children showing themselves up by being sulky and irritable. And what if Spike got carsick? He wasn't accustomed to travelling on anything but his own four legs.

She sipped a mug of strong black coffee, savouring the flavour of the freshly-ground beans, and tried not to think about the outing, or any underlying issues that may or may not be connected to it. A faint sound from above told her that the twins were up and moving. That was a good sign. If they were as miserable as they seemed, they would be far more inclined to stay in bed with headphones on.

Janie was like her mother. She loved listening to music. Although Tim liked music — not that he would admit to it — he was a typical boy and spent a lot of time playing computer games. And when they were displeased with Lara, the music and the games got played beneath the sheets. It was their odd way of making a statement, she supposed.

With one eye on the clock and one ear cocked to monitor the sounds upstairs, Lara made a selection of sandwiches to take with them to the beach. They would have a picnic at lunchtime, then Desmond planned to call in at a restaurant on the way home later on. He knew a good pizza place, apparently.

'Janie! Tim!' She called out to them as she packed sandwiches, fruit and drinks in a gaily-striped cool bag. 'Come on. Breakfast!'

She heard a scuffle going on above her head and a good amount of muttering, which made her frown suspiciously at the ceiling. However, they came running seconds later with excited grins on their faces and ate a good breakfast.

'Well, that's better,' Lara told them as she cleared away the dishes. 'Now, go and get the things you're taking for the day — cozzies, flip-flops, handkerchief . . . '

'Oh, Mum,' Jane complained. 'We're not babies any more. We're nearly eleven.'

'Ten and a quarter, anyway,' Tim chipped in.

'How long are you going to treat us like children?' Janie, her arms folded across her still flat chest, looked very adult and too worldly wise for Lara's comfort.

'Till you're at least thirty-two,' she told them with a grin. 'Go pack your bags.'

'My bag's been packed since last night,' Janie informed her.

'Mine, too,' Tim said, nodding his head gravely.

'Well, that's good. I was afraid you were going to be late and keep Desmond and his children waiting.'

'No . . . ' Janie said, stringing out the word as if it were a mile long.

'Why would we do that?' Tim wanted to know.

Lara shook her head at them, then gasped when she saw the bulging bags they had waiting in the hall. It looked as if they were taking everything but the kitchen sink with them in their backpacks.

'Good gracious, you don't need all that stuff,' she told them and they exchanged curious glances. 'We're only going for the day, you know . . . '

But there wasn't time to argue or to make them extract the unnecessary from their bags. Desmond was already drawing up outside the house in his car and tooting for them to join him.

Somehow, she didn't think he was the type to appreciate tardiness. Everything about him spoke of efficiency. She hoped he wasn't in for too much of a cultural shock with her small but disorganised family.

The four children greeted each other with restraint. Desmond, dressed conservatively for a day at the beach, inspected her strappy, floral dress and smiled his approval, though Spike received an unfriendly frown, which put his hackles up.

'Perhaps we'd better leave the poor old boy with Betty up the road,' Lara suggested, and dragged Spike off to her neighbour's house.

'I hope you've all brought your costumes,' Desmond said five minutes later as he started up the car and they set off.

Lara had stuck her old one-piece bathing suit in her bag at the last minute, but she wasn't sure whether she would be putting it on. Desmond was still very new in her life and she was self-conscious with him.

Anyway, she had put on a bit of weight and the costume might not even fit her any more.

If there were to be more visits to the seaside, she would have to invest in a new one.

She noticed that the twins seemed unusually quiet during the journey, only speaking when spoken to. From time to time, she glanced over her shoulder and tried to will them to chill out and enjoy the day. But her powers of maternal telepathy were not working on this occasion.

When they finally arrived at the coast they found it crowded and had to drive around for some time before they could find a place to park. Fortunately, where they ended up was near to the promenade, which pleased the children because there were things to do other than sunbathe and swim.

Since it was already past midday, they found a convenient flat rock and Lara set out the picnic things.

'You've gone to a lot of trouble, Lara,' Desmond said, tucking into a chicken leg. 'This is excellent. Better than tuna sandwiches, eh, kids?'

'Mum makes lovely tuna sandwiches,' Polly, his daughter said, with a sulky pout.

Lara heard Desmond's sigh and saw his pained expression.

'I'm afraid we're having one of our difficult weekends,' he told her tightly and fixed both his children with a no-nonsense paternal eye. 'Come on, you two. Enter into the spirit of things. Go on, Jason, have another chicken leg. Lara's brought enough to feed an army. And Polly, have some bread and cheese. It's good for you.'

'I don't like cheese,' Polly complained, staring glumly at the food spread out on the red and white tablecloth between them.

'Since when?' Desmond asked, taken aback.

'I've never liked cheese,' his daughter insisted and her father groaned.

'That reminds me of two other people I know,' Lara laughed and caught reprimanding expressions on the faces of her own two children.

'Can we go and get some chips, Dad?' Jason asked, already on his feet. 'There's a shop at the other end of the prom that sells super ones.'

'I suppose so,' Desmond gave in, anxious to keep the atmosphere sweet; he handed Jason some money. 'Bring some back for us. All right, Lara?'

'All right,' Lara nodded and watched Jason and Polly rush off on their mission.

What she did not expect was that the twins would get up and start out after Polly and Jason.

'Hey, where are you going? It doesn't take four of you to fetch the chips.'

'It's all right, Mum,' Janie replied, still walking away and with Tim close behind her. 'We just want to see what the place is like. Be back soon.'

'Why are you . . . ?' But Lara's question was never finished, for they were already out of earshot.

She turned to Desmond. 'Why on earth are they taking their backpacks?'

'They're your children,' he said with

a curious frown. 'I have enough problems trying to understand my own.'

Then, leaning his back against a rock, he closed his eyes and turned his face up to the sun. She hadn't taken him for a sun worshipper, but maybe she had been wrong about a lot of things concerning Desmond.

7

It took about fifteen minutes for the chips to arrive, but only Jason and Polly brought them. The twins were nowhere to be seen.

'Where are Janie and Tim?' Lara asked, scanning the beach with squinting eyes beneath a hand raised to ward off the sun's glare. 'Didn't they find you?'

Jason and Polly looked at her blankly. 'No,' Jason said slowly. 'Were they supposed to find us?'

'Well, yes . . . ' Lara got to her feet and dusted off the sand from her hands and her skirt. 'Are you sure you didn't see them?'

They shook their heads negatively, then started hungrily into the chips. A strong smell of grease, salt and vinegar wafted into the air all around them and a hopeful seagull swooped down low

85

with a keen eye on anything that might be thrown their way.

'Desmond . . . ?'

'Oh, sit down and eat your chips while they're still warm, Lara,' he said. 'They'll be all right. They probably just missed Jason and Polly.'

'They couldn't have missed us, Dad,' Jason said, his mouth full of chicken and chips. 'It's a straight walk from here. Look, you can see the shop there with the red awning.'

'Well, they won't have gone far, will they?' He addressed his question at Lara, who wasn't sure what to think. 'I mean, are they prone to running away and getting lost?'

She blinked at him, irritation mingling with a growing concern for her babies. No, that was silly. Janie and Tim were not babies any longer, but they were still very young. And this was no longer a world where children of any age were safe.

'I'll just wander down there,' she said. 'They might have got side-tracked by something or other.'

'Well, if you must,' Desmond said, helping himself to more bread and throwing a chunk of it to the seagull, which swooped on it as if it were starving. 'But I still think you're over-reacting.'

★ ★ ★

Half-an-hour had passed since the children had left. Lara wandered up and down the prom twice, looking in every shop, darting in and out of amusement arcades. She even stopped one or two people and asked if they had seen two children wearing identical orange and blue backpacks. No-one had.

'Blast them!' Desmond swore when she suggested that they had better go to the police. 'This was supposed to be a nice, enjoyable day. It looks as if we're fated not to get to know one another.'

Lara was shaking. The twins were not usually stupid. They did not go in for running away from home or any of the typical pranks that children and young teenagers got up to. They were, in fact, surprisingly responsible little human beings.

'There'll be other days, Desmond,' she said stiffly. 'Right now, my priority is to find my children.'

'They could be anywhere by now. Where do you suggest we start?'

'You stay there, in case they come back — please.'

'Oh, for goodness sake . . . '

Not liking his tone and his apparently uncaring attitude, Lara picked up her bag, slung it on her shoulder and went off in search of the nearest police station. She had to ask directions on the way, but she found it without too much difficulty and arrived at the station feeling and looking pale and agitated.

'My children . . . ' she gasped at the desk sergeant who looked up from filling in a crossword puzzle as she entered. 'I — I think they must be lost.'

The policeman listened to her kindly,

scribbled down some details — what Tim and Janie looked like, what they were wearing when last seen. It was the sort of thing you see on the telly and think will never happen to you.

'Right, now, Mrs — er ... ' He peered at his form, then looked up at her. 'Mrs Grainger, is it?'

Lara nodded, dumb now that she had blurted out all her fears and described her children from top to tail.

'Right, lass. I'll just see if there's a squad car available and they can take you round with them. Would you like a cup of tea first, eh?'

'No — thank you. I just want to find my children.'

Time and incidents were soon leapfrogging over one another and Lara felt almost as if she were being beamed here, there and everywhere. First a ride up and down the main streets of the town, then they went farther afield, keeping in radio contact with the station at all times.

Once, she thought she glimpsed Tim

and Janie, but it turned out to be two children with similar backpacks hurrying to catch up with a group of ramblers. Lara's hopes were fading fast, but she pushed the frightening, negative thoughts to the back of her mind, telling herself over and over that if she got them back safe and sound she would never let them out of her sight again.

It was a ridiculous promise, but that was how she felt. She would gladly sacrifice her life for those two wonderful kids.

There was a static crackle on the car radio. The policewoman, sitting in the front passenger seat leaned forward, glancing at her companion, who shook his head, then asked the caller to repeat the message.

Lara strained to hear the fractured voice and her heart leapt when she heard the words 'found them . . . ' The rest was too garbled and the car engine too loud to hear more. Besides, her ears were ringing and she hardly dared think.

'Wh — what did they say?' she demanded breathlessly. 'Did they say they've found them?'

The policewoman turned and beamed her a triumphant smile. 'Panic over, Mrs Grainger. They're safe and well and with their father, apparently.'

'What! But where . . . ?'

'Is that a surprise to you, Mrs Grainger?' PC Bolton was frowning at her.

Lara thought about it, then gave a little shake of her head. She pulled out her handkerchief and dried her tear-soaked cheeks.

'Yes and no,' she said. 'My husband and I are separated. The children don't even know him . . .'

'Not to worry. He's taking them back home. Where would you like us to drop you?'

Lara blinked at the question, then remembered that she had been with Desmond and his children before the twins disappeared. He must be good and worried by now, she thought. Or extremely angry. Somehow, she thought that the latter would be his most likely reaction.

'I left a friend and his children at the beach,' she said with difficulty, her voice still shaking as she waited for relief to sink in. 'Near the end of the pier. Would you mind?'

'No problem, luv,' the other young constable said and did an illegal U-turn in the middle of the busy afternoon traffic, causing a few hastily applied brakes, and, no doubt, some abusive language in surrounding traffic.

When Lara rejoined Desmond she could see by his tight expression that he was more concerned for the safety of the twins than he had let on.

'I'm so sorry, Desmond,' she said and he smiled and kissed her lightly on the cheek, then indicated Jason and Polly, who were sitting on the sand looking miserable.

'I've just been lecturing them about the evil of making parents suffer,' he said with a grimace. 'God, Lara, I'm so pleased your two came to no harm. I was steeling myself against a possible bad news thing, you know.'

'Yes, well . . . ' Lara looked at him apologetically. 'They're going to be even more miserable now, because I'm going to have to ask you to take me back home. Martin's taking the twins back there now.'

He looked at her reflectively, then shrugged. It was almost a defeatist attitude, but then it had been a fraught day for all of them.

'Let's just take one day at a time,' he said, then stalked off, leaving her to clear up their picnic things, watched sullenly by Jason and Polly.

'I'm sorry,' she told them. 'Really, I am.'

They shrugged and followed their father, leaving her to bring up the rear.

8

They arrived back at Lara's place at the same time as a taxi drew up with Martin and the twins in the back. The two cars parked nose to nose, the occupants of both peering forward uncertainly.

'Well, there you are, Lara,' Desmond said with a wry smile. 'Your baby birds back at the nest, plus one fledgling husband.'

She didn't trust herself to respond. It was obvious that he was far from pleased with the way the day had turned out. She couldn't blame him, but the circumstances were a little bizarre, by anybody's reckoning.

As she stepped out of the car, she smiled ruefully at Jason and Polly, sitting morosely in the back seat. They stared back at her. In the back of the taxi, Tim and Janie looked pretty much the same.

Only Martin was making the effort to look friendly as he got out. He raised his shoulders and spread his hands.

'Lara, I'm sorry about this,' he said. 'You must have been frantic.'

While he was getting the twins out of the taxi, Lara turned to Desmond and saw that he was giving Martin a lot of attention.

When she leaned into the car and touched his arm, he jumped slightly and turned melancholy eyes in her direction.

'Desmond, thank you so much — and I'm sorry — again. I'll give you a ring, shall I?'

There was just a touch of a negative air about him as he nodded and, without preamble, started turning the car, leaving her in the road, staring after him. She gave a sigh and turned her attention back to her children, who were already standing on the doorstep, waiting with fearful expressions on their young faces.

Before Lara could join them, Martin

was there at her side, his fingers finding and gripping her wrist, which made her tingle from head to foot and she wished he had not touched her.

'Don't be too hard on them, Lara,' he said. 'What they did was all in a worthy cause.'

'Really? Whose?'

'Yours — and mine.' He smiled and suddenly the world seemed brighter, just as it had all those years ago when she had fallen in love with him. 'Theirs too.'

'I have no doubt that they thought they were doing the right thing, Martin, but the truth is they gave me a few hours of absolute terror and I'm quite inclined to beat the living daylights out of them.'

Lara spoke loudly so that the twins could hear every word and she saw them flinch and exchange what she had long ago named their 'telepathic look'. Sometimes she really did believe that they shared the same brain. They certainly seemed to be tuned in to one another's thoughts, which at times was quite scary.

With Tim and Janie installed in their living-room and Martin hovering restlessly behind the sofa where they sat, Lara let them know, in no uncertain terms, the trouble they were in.

'Have you any idea how much I worried when you didn't come back after half an hour? What possessed you to go off like that?'

Again the two sets of identical eyes met, held, then looked at her. She noticed that they were holding hands, tightly, as if afraid of her and that made her feel bad. She had hardly ever done more than raise her voice to them on very rare occasions. What must Martin be thinking of her right now, she wondered? What kind of mother did he think she was?

Her shoulders slumping, she sank down in her favourite chair and regarded them.

'Oh, for goodness sake, take that look off your faces,' she pleaded, her eyes sliding over to Martin and back again. 'You know I'm not going to beat you, though right now that's exactly what I feel I should be doing.'

'Oh, Mum!' Tim looked at her sideways, scowling.

'We just thought . . . ' Janie started to speak, but then stopped, uncertain how to continue. She looked at her brother. 'You can tell her.'

'No, you!'

Then the pair of them turned and looked pleadingly at their father. 'All right,' he said. 'I'll explain things, but don't expect your mother to understand. From the look of her, she's ready to beat all three of us black and blue.'

His words raised a tentative smile all round, even from Lara, who was finding it difficult to act the role of big, bad mother, no matter how much they had worried her.

'I'll go put the kettle on, shall I, Mum,' Janie suggested.

'And I'll get the biscuits,' Tim added.

They were doing their best to winkle

their way out of trouble. Her initial response was to make them stay and sit out the discussion with Martin, but they looked so downcast and remorseful she relented and let them go.

'So this is what it's like, raising my children,' Martin said with the hint of a twinkle in his dark eyes.

Feeling a rise of suffocating emotion, Lara paced the floor in front of him, uncomfortably aware that he followed her every move closely, appraising her, comparing her, no doubt, with the Lara he had once known.

'I've had no problems with them so far,' she told him and saw his lips twitch, but he suppressed the ready smile that had once been the undoing of her.

'Not until I appeared on the scene,' he said repentantly. 'Is that it?'

'Something like that, yes.' She paced some more, then, when he remained silently watching her, she threw her hands in the air and flopped down opposite him. 'Have you any idea,

Martin, what it's like trying to raise two children without a father? I know many women do it these days, but not many of them were left so high and dry as I was. Do you know what that did to me?'

He sucked in his breath, placed his fingers together and stared long and hard at the tent it made.

'Don't think I haven't thought about it, Lara. There's not a year — a month or a week gone by that you haven't been in my mind. Not a day when I haven't castigated myself for the way I behaved.'

Their eyes met, but neither of them seemed to be capable of saying more at that particular moment in time. From the kitchen came the sound of clattering dishes as the twins made tea. Somewhere in the garden the fluted song of a blackbird filled the heady air and a waft of rose perfume permeated the room through an open window.

After a while, Martin got to his feet and stood, his back to her, staring out at the neat garden.

'Do you have someone to do the garden for you?' he asked, probably in order to break the icy silence.

'Not really,' she said, her voice weak in her throat, her body feeling limp and heavy. 'I take care of most of it. When there's any heavy work needed there are one or two neighbours who are willing to lend a hand.'

He threw her an interested glance over his shoulder. 'Especially the men, no doubt.'

She gave him a reproachful frown, which he didn't see because he had turned his attention back to her garden.

'Not the way you mean,' she told him pointedly. 'They're mostly married and very respectable. Or unmarried and very young.'

He turned to face her then. 'I apologise, Lara. There was no call for that remark — about the men, I mean. If you have other men running after you, I can hardly complain, can I? In fact, I wouldn't blame you, not after what happened between us.'

Hoping she sounded casual, Lara forced out a question that had been nagging her.

'What about you, Martin? Have you had anyone special in your life?'

She held her breath, waiting for his response. It was odd, because she couldn't make up her mind what she wanted to hear. Would things get easier for her if he had someone? Surely, in ten years, he must have met plenty of women.

'I have women friends,' he said, after a long silence. 'Friends, acquaintances — but since you ask, no, I don't have anyone special.'

There it was, that little flip of her heart. It was a sensation she wished she had not felt. She couldn't afford to have feelings where Martin was concerned.

This, she kept reminding herself, was the man who had left her stranded, high and dry, ten years ago, and had not been in touch until now. She should hate him, but she wasn't the type of person who could hate too easily. And Martin wasn't the kind of person anyone could hate.

Well, that's what she thought when she met him, and when she married him. There were times, however, when friends and family had told her that she was well rid of him. That was after he had disappeared from her life. And she had almost believed them.

She had to have some hate in her heart at that time, in order to survive the ordeal of being a single mother without the support of the man she loved.

9

'What happened, Martin?' she asked now, her voice so low even she could hardly hear the words.

For a moment she thought he had not heard her, but then he turned to face her and she saw agonies, like dark thunderclouds, flitting over his face. He came to sit opposite her, placed his hands together in a praying position and pressed his forefingers to his trembling lips.

'I was nineteen,' he said, speaking to the floor between them as his mind searched for the right words to say. 'Not very mature, really, although I thought I was quite adult. I had gone from boyhood to manhood in one very big, very quick step. There I was, in love so much that the only thing that mattered was to marry you in order to keep you.'

He glanced up and she saw that his

eyes had misted over. He gave a few rapid blinks and tightened his mouth.

'Go on, Martin,' Lara said. 'I'm listening.'

'We were so good together, Lara,' he continued. 'I had never known anything so good in my life before I met you — and certainly not since. They say that most people have doubts before they get married. I never had any doubts about you or our life together. Not once.'

'And yet you left me, Martin, when I needed you most,' Lara reminded him, a catch in her throat.

'Please — let me finish.'

'All right. I suppose I owe you that much.'

His eyes flickered over her and she gave him what must have seemed a funny little smile that was meant to be encouraging, but her deeper emotions were getting in the way and it would only take a snap of the fingers for her to dissolve into tears of absolute misery.

'Thank you. I know you think I don't

deserve any kindnesses from you — and you're right. But I want you to know how I felt — know what made me run away.'

Lara said nothing. She fixed her eyes on her hands, nestling limply together in her lap. This had to be one of the hardest moments of her life so far. Perhaps it was the same for Martin.

Now, his fingers were interlocked, his whitened knuckles brushing his chin. She noticed, for the first time, that he still wore the wedding ring she had given him, exchanging it with hers at the altar the day they got married.

Lara heard his long, indrawn breath and waited for him to go on. She felt like she was judge and jury hearing the testimony of the accused, but she wasn't unbiased. She had already found him guilty years ago. It was unlikely she would change her mind now.

'At nineteen,' Martin said, 'we're supposed to be adults. We can vote, hold down responsible jobs, take out mortgages and loans, go to war and die for our country.'

Another glance to check that she was, in fact, taking all this in; she gave a small nod. 'We're physically strong, intellectually bright. It's only our emotions that haven't grown up with us. We're still children in our hearts. Children who get out of their depth, get concerned, terrified by the new world they suddenly find themselves in.

'When you told me you were pregnant, Lara, I was so shocked at the thought of being a father so soon in our lives together — well, I panicked. I couldn't control it, didn't know how I felt, didn't know where to turn. So I did the cowardly thing. I ran away.'

He looked directly at her and she saw that there were tears streaming down his cheeks. It took her by surprise. It was, at the same time, embarrassing and very moving. But he could still speak, even though he was choking on his words.

'I knew I was doing an unforgivable thing, that all I needed was time to get used to the idea. I knew that with your help, because we loved each other so much, I would succeed. And still, I couldn't bring myself to come back to you. I wrote letters, but you never replied. I don't know why I expected you to — and that's when I got a solicitor to send you divorce papers, but you didn't respond to them either.'

'I didn't even read them,' Lara told him, remembering that one contact was so impersonal. 'I kept putting it off. My head was too full of losing the one person who had meant the world to me. It was full of being deserted while I was pregnant, full of having not just one baby, but two inside me, and you weren't there with me.'

'I phoned your mother from France, did you know? No, I suppose she wouldn't tell you.'

'Tell me what?'

'That I wanted a second chance, that I wanted — no, needed, to spend the rest of my life with you and be a father to our child.'

'I can imagine what she said to that,' Lara said, her eyes flashing angrily as she thought of her manipulative mother, always bent on having things her way, with total disregard for her daughter's feelings.

'She told me that there was no baby, that you had . . . ' He gulped audibly, continuing with the greatest difficulty. 'She said that you had lost the baby.'

'Oh, my God, she didn't! I don't believe it . . . ' But Lara did believe it. Lies were Evelyn's stock in trade.

She shook her head and fought against the constricting lump that had risen in her own throat.

'I got the papers from the solicitor,' she told him huskily. 'But I never got your letters. I know now that my mother destroyed them. She didn't want me to be hurt any more than I was already.'

'Oh, God, Lara, why didn't you divorce me?'

'I couldn't. I thought — there was always a chance . . . ' She couldn't go

109

on and suddenly he was down on his knees before her, his hands gripping hers.

'Can you ever forgive me, Lara?' She stared at him, trembling, feeling that she should tell him to leave, wanting him to stay, 'They say that leopards can't change their spots, but if you'll give me half a chance, I'd like to try and make it up to you for the lost years — and the lost love.'

Lara's lips clamped tightly together. Whatever she said right now would be wrong. How could she commit herself one way or the other when her head was at war with her heart and they had reached a terrible stalemate?

10

'Right now, Martin,' Lara said thickly, when she could find enough voice, 'my brain refuses to function. I think you should just go.'

'Do you mean go, as in forever, or just leave you to think things over?'

Lara's brows knitted and she drew up her shoulders. 'I don't know what I mean,' she said, frustration eating away at her nerves.

'Lara, for ten years I believed you hated me, thought you'd lost my baby, thought you never wanted to see or hear from me again. I suspect that it wasn't that way at all. Your mother wasn't in favour of us getting married. My running off in a panic gave her all the fuel she needed to keep us apart.'

Lara sighed. 'I'm sure she believed she was doing it for the best. Mothers are like that. They never consider that they may be ruining lives.'

Martin stood up, shoved his hands in his trouser pockets and looked about him at Lara's small, but tidy sitting-room.

'It looks like you rose above it all,' he said. 'You have every reason to be proud of yourself.'

'I've learned how to be independent, Martin.' Lara, too, got to her feet. 'Will you go back to France?'

The question seemed to shake him. Perhaps it told him something she had not been able to voice — that she did not want him to stay, did not want him to mess up her life a second time.

'Eventually, yes, but I'm on holiday at the moment, so I'll be around for a week or two.'

'Please go,' Lara whispered, her lips starting to tremble uncontrollably.

He blinked, nodded, headed for the door. She wondered if his legs felt as weak as hers did at that moment. Was his head full of clouds, his brain all but dead?

They walked together in silence to the front door. She let him open it because her hands were shaking too much. He pulled it back and hesitated on the step.

'Lara, please let me see the twins before I go back to France. Even if you don't want me, our children need to know that they have a father who cares. I want to get to know them, to be their father. Or am I asking too much of you?'

'I think maybe you are, Martin.' Tears were already stinging Lara's eyes. She blinked them away furiously, then said in a small croaking voice: 'We'll just have to see.'

She closed the door quickly behind him and forced herself not to go to a window to watch him walk away.

★　★　★

'Nice to see you back on your feet again,' Desmond said with a warm smile. 'How are you feeling?'

113

In the two weeks that had followed her last encounter with Martin, Lara had come down with summer flu. She had been particularly poorly and the doctor had declared that she was run down and perhaps suffering from emotional stress. It wasn't unknown, he told her in a fatherly fashion, for young single mothers to succumb to germs from time to time.

Desmond had phoned, in yet another vain attempt to fix a family outing. On hearing that she was ill, he took it upon himself to take all four children on outings, then came round and fussed about her like a mother hen.

The schools were all closed for the summer and he had taken his annual leave so he could spend some quality time with Jason and Polly. And, she suspected, with her. Just when she needed to be taken out of herself and away from the situation with Martin, she fell ill.

'I'm much better, thank you, Desmond,' she told him with a bright smile and he put a finger under her chin and studied her face closely.

'Hmm. Still a bit pale around the gills,' he said. 'And what are those shadows under your eyes? Aren't you sleeping?'

'Not very well,' she said. 'The doctor's given me some sleeping tablets, but I don't like using them. The trouble is, with the twins at home all the time, full of energy, I don't get much rest. Then by the time they've gone to bed, I just lie staring at the ceiling, thinking . . . '

She blushed, knowing that she was on the point of telling him too much. This new man in her life did not wish to hear that her thoughts were constantly haunted by her estranged husband. What he did want to hear was that she was ready to go out with him, on a proper date — not just a family outing. She felt that she owed him that, at least.

'I had your mother come into my office the other day,' Desmond said as he went about the sitting-room, picking up the clutter the twins had left lying around and she hadn't yet got round to tidying away. 'You know, you really should make Tim and Janie clear away after themselves, Lara.'

'They're usually very good,' she said in their defence. 'I don't know what's got into them lately. They're restless, moody and — well, I don't seem to have enough incentive to chase after them. It's been a difficult time for all three of us.'

'Correction — all four of us.' He sat down beside her and placed a hand casually on her knee. 'Do you feel up to going out for dinner this evening? My sister will babysit all four kids, so there's no problem there.'

Lara licked her lips and fixed her eyes on his hand, not sure whether she liked it there or not. He removed it quickly and cleared his throat as he waited for her reply.

'What did my mother have to say for herself, then?' she asked. 'Or is that an

116

indiscreet question? I mean, she is your client and I understand all about ethical practice, but since you mentioned it first . . . '

'She was mainly concerned about you,' he said, wringing out a smile that did not quite make it to his eyes; smiling was not something he did readily, she had found.

'Well, if it's about me, then it's probably my mother who is being indiscreet,' she said, huffily. 'So, what did she want?'

Desmond shrugged and placed the games and toys he had collected in a corner of the room. 'She was asking how we were getting along,' he told her carefully, his eyes flitting over her, but not holding her gaze for more than a second. 'I gather you and she had a bit of a row.'

Lara tossed her head and gave a snorting laugh of derision. 'That's an understatement,' she told him, fresh anger rising up in her as she was reminded of how her mother had interfered in her life and been the cause of such unnecessary suffering.

'She also wanted to be sure that you were not seeing Martin.'

'I'm not seeing Martin,' she said, and the smile she gave him almost hurt. 'There you are. You can report back to her.'

'I'm not spying on you, Lara,' he said stiffly. 'Please don't think that. After all, I have a vested interest too. One of these days we might even succeed in going out together without your past life getting in the way.'

'Maybe,' she said, her forehead furrowing deeply. 'But not just yet, Desmond, please.'

'Still not one hundred per cent, eh?'

'Something like that. Maybe, when things get back to normal . . . '

He was studying her again and she didn't like it, because it made her feel guilty.

'OK, but keep it in mind, eh?' He leaned over her and planted an unexpected kiss on her cheek. 'In the meantime, how would you like me to take the twins off your hands for a week. I've rented a house by the sea. It comes equipped with everything growing adolescents might need — tennis court, pool, television, computers. They'll love it. When they're not enjoying themselves on the beach they can drive me mad inside the house instead of you. How about it?'

'Oh, Desmond, it's very kind of you, but . . . '

'You can come along too, if you feel up to it, but I thought maybe you would benefit more from a few days of total isolation. They say it's good for the soul.'

She gave him a little laugh. 'Do they?'

11

In the end, Lara was persuaded that Desmond was right. The twins, displaying mixed feelings, were packed off to the seaside with assurances that if they did not enjoy it they could come home immediately.

For the first few hours, Lara wandered aimlessly about the house feeling that there was a great big hole in the middle of her existence. She had never been separated from her children, though she had often dreamed of one day having more time to herself. It was a dream that made her feel totally selfish, yet she was sensible enough to accept that a little independence was necessary for everybody.

The following morning she was gritting her teeth, telling herself that if she telephoned Desmond so soon after their departure, he might see it as a neurotic mother syndrome. She didn't think she was particularly neurotic when it came to her children, just concerned for their wellbeing. Lara was determined never to treat Tim and Janie the way her own mother had treated her.

Outside, the sun was shining, the air was fresh. Lara decided to go for a walk, which was always a popular choice with Spike. They returned invigorated and she was in the garden contemplating the numerous jobs that were outstanding when the telephone rang.

'Desmond!' She cradled the telephone between ear and shoulder as she struggled to pull off her gardening gloves, shedding soil over her feet and the floor. 'Is everything all right?'

'Yes, of course.' Desmond laughed in her ear. 'Stop worrying. They're having a whale of a time. I just wanted to warn you that we may go out for the odd day or two, so don't get twitchy if you can't reach us by phone.'

'Don't solicitors carry mobiles these days?' she asked.

'Well, yes, but I tend to switch mine off when I'm on holiday. Look, if you absolutely insist, I'll give you a ring every evening to let you know that your babies are safe and well and still on this planet.'

Lara mulled his suggestion over and decided, at the risk of him thinking her silly, she would prefer a little regular contact after all.

'If it's not too much trouble, I think I would like that, Desmond.'

'I would like it better if you would simply like to hear my voice.'

Lara juggled with the phone as it slipped. She took a moment to reflect on the inference in his words. He was openly flirting with her. It shouldn't bother her, but it did. It made her feel vaguely uncomfortable.

'I'm always pleased to hear your voice, Desmond,' she said with a light laugh that she hoped did not sound too forced.

'I'm very glad about that, Lara.'

His voice had dropped very low and sounded thick in his throat. Lara tensed up, glad he was at the other end of a telephone wire and not there in the room beside her. If things were starting to happen between them, she didn't want it to proceed too quickly. Already, she was aware of an invisible finger hovering over her personal panic button.

Once bitten, twice shy, she heard her mother's favourite phrase echoing in her head. Well, perhaps Evelyn was correct in that, at least.

'Let's just leave it at that for the time being, shall we?' she said quickly and a little breathlessly into the mouthpiece. 'You'll ring me?'

'Anything you say, Lara.'

★   ★   ★

Desmond kept his word and rang Lara every evening after the children had gone to bed. Just listening to his voice and knowing that the twins were all right and still enjoying themselves, put her mind at rest. She was even beginning to sleep better, though her sleep was punctuated by disturbing dreams that stayed with her long after she woke up.

When her neighbour, Betty, came round for coffee one morning, she poured out a lot of things that she had been keeping bottled up. Betty was a bit of a rough diamond, but she had a heart of gold and always had a sympathetic ear. For the first time, Lara told her about Martin turning up out of the blue. Until now, no one but her mother had known this fact.

'I don't believe it!' Betty squealed ecstatically. 'He actually wrote in to one of those soppy love song programmes? Oh, God, I would have died if it had been me. And your kids writing to him behind your back. But how romantic, Lara.'

'Yes, I suppose it is,' Lara agreed, grudgingly. 'Martin always was a born romantic. That's what I loved about him most of all. I just wish it had never happened. It's brought back too many painful memories.'

'What's he like now, then?' Betty was all agog. 'Is he still as dishy as you remember him?'

Lara laughed. 'I suppose you could still call him dishy,' she said, her stomach churning slightly as a mental image of Martin materialised inside her head. 'He's put on some weight — muscle mainly. And because he lives in France, he has a definite cosmopolitan air about him.'

'Ooh, all muscular and bronzed, eh? You lucky thing to have him still in love with you.'

'Oh, but . . . ' Lara shook her head. 'It's not like that, Betty. I mean, I can't — not after what he did — walking away like that.'

'But you said yourself it was mainly your mother's fault. If she was my mother I'd want to kill her.'

'And — well, there's somebody else,'

Lara faltered and saw her friend's look of surprise. 'It's not serious or anything. Not yet. We've only just met, but . . . '

'But?'

'I think I like him,' Lara sighed, relieved to be able to talk openly about Desmond and her feelings. 'I didn't at first, but I think that was because my mother introduced us. You know what she's like about pushing me towards any eligible male that comes her way.'

Betty nodded. 'I'm surprised you're still single. How have you stood it all these years, Lara? Doesn't the loneliness get to you?'

Lara thought deeply and drew in a profound breath before letting it out slowly.

'Yes, of course it does, but having the twins helps. And dear old Spike. And now — there's Desmond. He's a solicitor.'

'Why do I get the feeling that you're not all that enthusiastic?'

Lara's eyebrows shot up. 'I thought that would be obvious. I don't want to get hurt again. Maybe I'll get more enthusiastic when I know him better. Up until now we haven't even managed a proper date.'

Betty got up and prepared to leave. She pressed a hand on Lara's shoulder and gave her one of her wise, all-knowing smiles that for once Lara found irritating.

'Did you know that when you mention Martin's name, your eyes light up? I wouldn't mind betting that his reappearance in your life has stirred up more than nostalgia.'

'Don't be ridiculous!'

12

After a hesitant start, Lara had enjoyed her first week without the children, learning what it was like to think just for herself. She even went to a concert, happy in the knowledge that Tim and Janie were in good hands and not being bored out of their skulls.

Now, however, she was beginning to miss them as the silence of the house gathered about her. And Spike was unusually subdued too.

During the week, she had made peace with her mother, though it was, as ever, built on shaky ground. Evelyn only became reasonable when Lara assured her that Martin was gone and they would probably never see or hear from him again.

'If you take him back, my girl,' Evelyn drummed into her, 'you'll never be able to trust him, mark my words.'

'What makes you think I'm taking him back, Mum?' Lara asked wearily, her patience wearing thin.

'You'd be a fool if you did.'

'I'm not even contemplating it.'

There was a short silence, then. 'Well, just as long as you remember that, Lara. You know, you'd do worse than marry Desmond. He's keen enough.'

'Mum, I wish you would stop meddling in my life!'

Before her mother could go on, Lara curtailed the conversation abruptly. Perhaps a little too abruptly, for the telephone rang almost as soon as she had replaced the receiver.

'I'm sorry, Mum . . . ' she began.

'What?'

'Who's this?' Lara realised the mistake she had made.

'Mum? It's Tim! Didn't you recognise my voice?'

'Tim! Are you all right? Nothing's happened to Janie, has it?'

Oh, goodness, there she was again,

being neurotic and over-protective. It had been all right up until now, but the twins were growing up fast and were of an age when they resented parental handling of the tight rein sort. She was going to have to be less obvious in her approach if she didn't want to alienate them.

'We're OK, Mum,' Tim said. 'It's just that . . . '

She listened and a short silence was followed by a whispered conversation that came to her too muffled to understand. Janie was obviously arguing some point or other with her brother.

'Mum, it's Janie! Stop it, Tim! Let me speak to Mum. You'll just go and ruin it.'

Lara braced herself. Intuition told her that her children were about to wrap her around their little fingers. Well, they would try, as they always did. Not always did they win, but she was prepared to listen to reasonable arguments.

'Janie, what is it?'

'It's nothing, honestly, Mum. Just Tim being silly.'

There was the sound of Tim being even sillier somewhere close to, and another sound in the background. Muted male voices.

'Who's there with you? Has Desmond got company?'

'It's just Desmond,' Janie said quickly. 'Mum, can we stay here another week? Please?'

'It's really wicked, here, Mum!' Tim shouted down the phone, and there was a rumble of sudden laughter, very grown-up laughter.

'Aren't you going to tell me who's there with you?' Lara asked.

'It's nobody,' Janie said, and from the disjointed, breathless tone of her voice, she was having to fight off her brother as she spoke. 'Just Jason and Polly — and Desmond. We're playing Scrabble just to please the grown-ups.'

Grown-ups. 'How many grown-ups

are there, Janie?' Lara quizzed her daughter.

'There's Desmond and there's — um — Desmond and Jason!'

'Put Desmond on, would you?'

Desmond, when he finally came on the line, sounded a little strange. It was almost as if he didn't want to speak to her.

'How are you, Lara?' he asked stiffly.

'Janie says they want to stay another week,' Lara said in a clipped tone, feeling that Desmond ought to have discussed the possibility with her before anything was decided with the children.

'Yes — errm — yes, that's right. You — ah — don't mind, do you?'

'Well, yes, actually. I do!' Lara squared her shoulders and frowned at her reflection in the mirror above the telephone table. 'I'm missing them. And I need to get them sorted out for going back to school in September.'

'Well, of course, I could bring them home tomorrow as originally planned,' Desmond said awkwardly, 'but they're having such a good time I don't want to spoil their fun.'

'Hmm. Maybe I could come and spend the day with you all. I could do with a breath of sea air.' Lara waited and all fell silent for far too long.

'Not a good idea, Lara,' Desmond told her. 'Trust me on this one, eh?'

Feeling like some kind of superfluous, extra limb, Lara drew in sufficient breath to singe Desmond's ear, but then he was gone and the twins were again speaking to her.

'You would hate it down here, Mum,' Janie said. 'It's not your kind of scene, you know, all that sand.'

It was true that Lara had never liked sand, but she loved being near the sea.

'It's all children, Mum,' Tim put his two-pennyworth in. 'There are millions of them.'

'Well, goodness, I know when I'm not wanted,' she said, trying to sound light-hearted, but what were her children doing, hurting her this way?

'See you in a week, Mum,' Janie said,

then the two of them were shouting goodbye in her ear and she didn't have time to say any more.

Lara went into the kitchen to make a cup of coffee, all the time telling herself that this was how it was when children were growing up. They needed their mothers less and less.

The trouble was, she didn't want them needing somebody else. Like Desmond. At least, not to the exclusion of their mother.

Feeling the need to speak to Desmond seriously about the situation, she tried phoning him back, but there was no answer on the number he had given her.

She tried her mother, but she was no help. Evelyn was only too delighted that things were 'progressing' between her daughter and her solicitor.

'Mum, it's hardly an affair, so don't go embroidering on top of the truth, will you — please?'

'Lara, you're a fool if you don't snap him up before someone else does,' her mother said sharply. 'Desmond is a very nice man and he needs a mother for those two children of his. I suppose he's told you that his ex-wife has remarried and is moving to Florida, leaving the children with him?'

'No, Mum, he hasn't told me that,' Lara said, feeling a sudden anger surge in her. And she thought, if all he wants me for is to be a mother to his children, he can forget that.

She quickly drew the conversation to an end, knowing from experience that it was safer than getting embroiled in yet another spat that would leave her feeling guilty and depressed.

As she replaced the receiver, she was aware of her back teeth gritting together so tightly her jaw was aching. How silly, she thought with a deep sigh and forced herself to relax.

But she still wasn't fully relaxed by the time there was a trill of the doorbell, followed by the sound of Betty's feet marching unceremoniously down the hall. Betty was a good friend and could always be called upon to baby-sit if Lara needed to go out in the evening.

She was the plump, motherly sort, always ready with wise advice, though she never presumed to force-feed anyone with her opinions.

'Hello, love,' she said, beaming all over her plump face and sinking down thankfully into an armchair. 'Ooh, that's better. Me feet're killing me.'

'Where've you been, Betty?' Lara asked, glad to have something to take her mind off the situation with the twins. 'You look as if you've caught a bit too much sun.'

'Aye, hinny, I have,' Betty gave a raucous laugh. 'Me and Tommy decided to have a day by the sea, but I got too hot. Anyway, we ended up walking about the town and eating fish and chips. Now, I'm done-in.'

'The twins are at the seaside. They're staying with a friend.'

'Aye, I was just going to tell you. We saw them,' Betty kicked off her shoes with a heartfelt groan and gave her feet a massage. 'They were having a great time and I couldn't help wondering where you were. That fella they were with — well, he was a bit of all right. He a friend, you say? Only, if he's not married, I'd move in quick, if I was you.'

'Desmond's divorced, but . . . '

'Oh, that's convenient, then. Lovely dark hair he's got and a smile to melt the knees beneath you . . . What's wrong, pet?'

Lara was staring at her friend, eyes wide, mouth hanging open.

'Desmond is fair,' she said. 'Are you sure it was Janie and Tim you saw?'

'Couldn't mistake them, love. Anyway, they waved to us as we passed. I didn't see no fair-haired man, but there was no mistaking who they were with. Handsome young fella, tall and muscular . . . '

Lara had gone cold. Betty was describing not Desmond, but Martin. What was Martin doing with the children? She thought he had gone back to France. And where in the world was Desmond in all this?'

'Betty, could you tell me exactly where you saw the twins?'

'Yes, love. It was on the Old Shore Road, the posh end where the houses have gardens right down to the beach almost. Most of the houses are summer lets these days.'

'And the children were near one of these houses?'

'Aye. In fact, they were in the garden. I remember the house well, because it was different. Red brick in parts instead of stone and there were roses climbing all over the walls — pink ones. Lovely looking place. I wouldn't mind spending a few days living in a house like that meself.'

'Betty, do you think Tommy's too tired to drive me down there?' Lara felt her blood sizzling in her veins from some kind of unnamed fear.

'He'll not want to miss Coronation Street, but . . . ' Betty struggled to her feet and came over to Lara. 'Here, love, you've gone very pale. Are you all right?'

'I'll be all right, Betty, when I've got my children back. Would you please ask Tommy to help me . . . ?'

Betty's husband was a little put out at being dragged away from his favourite soap, but when he saw Lara's agitated state, he softened and was sweetness itself on the hour's drive to the sea.

'Here we are, pet,' as he pulled up in front of an imposing house that exactly matched Betty's description. 'Those two imps of yours were in the garden there with a fella that might have been their dad.'

Might have been their dad, indeed. How would dear old Tommy react, Lara wondered, if she told him that the person in question was the twins' father? What would he think of a man who had ignored his children since before they were born, and now . . . What was Martin playing at? Was he planning to steal the twins, take them back to France? What?

'Thank you, Tommy,' she said, giving his hand a squeeze. 'I won't be long.'

'Take your time, lass,' he said with a kindly nod. 'I'll be here when you need me.'

Lara strode boldly up the garden path and, ignoring the bell-push, banged loudly on the door with her clenched fist. Somewhere inside the house, things were happening. A television picture flashed at her through the glass of the large bay window and muffled sounds wafted out on the evening air. In a neighbouring garden somewhere, a dog barked.

It seemed to take a long time and a second banging on the door before footsteps sounded in the hall. She counted every slapping footfall on what must be a tiled floor. The owner of the feet was whistling merrily. Childish laughter — Tim and Janie's — could be heard joining in with a television audience. Everything sound so normal and — oh, so happy.

The door in front of her opened and suddenly she was face to face with Martin. He was surprised to see her, that was obvious. Surprised and a little uncomfortable.

'Lara!' he exclaimed and took an involuntary step back.

'What have you done with my children?' she shouted in his face and, before he had the chance to reply, she bought the flat of her hand sharply across his face. 'How dare you steal them from me! After all these years when we didn't know if you were dead or alive.

'Years when you didn't care one way or the other about your children — or me!'

'Oh, Lara,' he said, not bothering about the slap, not bothering to hide the tears that sprang to his eyes. 'How wrong you are!'

13

'What are you doing here?' Lara demanded of Martin. 'You have a lot of explaining to do, Martin! And where is Desmond?'

'Don't be tough on Desmond,' Martin said as he followed her into the house. 'He just thought he was doing us both a favour.'

'A favour? How could he see it that way, allowing you to steal my children from me?'

'I'm not really stealing them,' Martin said quietly, opening a door and indicating for her to enter. 'And they are my children, after all.'

'How could Desmond do this to me!'

'Maybe because he saw something that you were incapable of seeing, Lara.'

Lara walked into the spacious living room and saw her children for the first time. They looked bronzed and healthy. And very happy to see her. They both rushed at her for a hug, then beamed at Martin, jumping up and down and hanging on to his brown, muscular arms.

'It worked!' Tim squeaked, frowning at his sister when she gave him a warning look. 'What?'

'Nothing, cabbage head!'

Tim fumed and Janie pulled a face at him before giving a nervous giggle.

'Would somebody please tell me what this is all about?' Lara asked, feeling weak and disorientated.

'Desmond's gone home, Mum,' Janie said, with another sharp glance at Martin. 'He said . . . '

She seemed to swallow her words as if they were too much for her to pronounce. Crossing in front of Martin, she stood, shoulder to shoulder, with her brother. Both looked sheepishly at the floor.

'Well?'

'He said . . . ' Martin took up the

story, stepping forward and taking her hand, which she wished he hadn't, because it felt so good. 'He said that, much as he regretted it, he was obviously not the man for you.'

'How could he tell?' Lara asked, feeling hot under the collar. 'We hardly had the opportunity to get to know one another.'

'I think, Lara,' said Martin, 'that he knew enough to realise that you and he were not exactly meant for one another. Whereas . . . '

'Whereas?'

Martin looked at the two children he had fathered and deserted before they were born. It had not been his fault that he didn't come back, she knew that now, but there was still some residual resentment hanging on.

She knew, also, how easy it must have been for a raw, nineteen-year-old to take fright at the thought of all the responsibilities marriage and parent-hood would bring. His flight might have been brief, had it not been for the well-meaning, but completely wrong interference of Evelyn, who 'said' she only wanted the best for her daughter.

Lara shook her head helplessly. They said you should never go back, that nothing would ever be the same if you did; that there would only be regrets waiting for you. Maybe, if Martin had come back to her years ago, it would have been different. Now, it was too late.

With a catch in her voice, she avoided Martin's hurt eyes as she ordered the children gently, but firmly, to collect their belongings. They were going home, she told them. It wasn't much, but it was all they had. And it wasn't going to get up and run off one day when least expected.

★   ★   ★

They saw the smoke long before they turned into the village. Too much billowing blue-grey cloud for somebody's garden rubbish. As they drew closer to their road, they saw flames too, heard fire engine sirens, saw people standing back, arms crossed about their chests, their faces stricken.

'Good God!' Tommy exclaimed, pulling up at the edge of the area that was cordoned off. 'Here, mate, what's happened? We live down there, river-side.'

The uniformed police officer, with his two-way phone chattering away busily, held up a hand and inspected Lara and the two children as they jumped out of the car.

'Are you the Grainger family, by any chance?'

Lara nodded, already feeling the blood drain from her face. The twins crowded in behind her. She could feel them gripping the material of her skirt, and feel their growing alarm.

The policeman looked relieved and spoke into his phone. 'They've just turned up, sir,' she heard him say. 'Two adults and two children.'

Tommy pushed forward and tugged

at the officer's sleeve.

'I'm Tommy Carter, their neighbour. Is my wife all right?'

Betty, they were all glad to hear, was all right. Lara's house had suddenly gone up in flames. It was all a bit confusing, but the firemen believed that there had been a short in the ancient electrical wiring.

When they were finally allowed near the ruined building that had been their home for a whole decade, there was nothing much left of it to salvage. Only one wall was left remaining. It was odd to see shelves and cupboards that had once housed their possessions, all charred and black.

'Isn't there anything left?' Tim wanted to know and Janie began to cry softly.

'Spike!' Lara suddenly remembered their dog. 'Where's Spike? Has anybody seen him?'

Faces turned away, heads shook. Nobody seemed capable of speaking to her. Then a strong arm wound its way about her shoulders and she looked up into Desmond's grey face.

'Oh, Desmond, I can't find Spike!' Lara tugged away from him.

'I came as soon as your mother phoned,' he said, following her closely as she plodded about in scorched, wet grass and rubble that still smouldered. 'She's in the car. Betty contacted her and we came right over.'

'I don't care about my mother!' Lara snapped out the cutting phrase, feeling immediately sorry for her words the moment they were out, but her mother was the least of her worries at that moment. 'I need to find my dog. Don't you understand?'

How could he understand? For ten years she had ploughed all her emotions, all her thoughts and dreams and fears, into that hairy hound, when there had been no one else to turn to. And he had given her unconditional love in return. Dear old Spike was precious to her. She could not afford to lose him now.

'Oh, Lara, pet, I'm so sorry!' Betty hugged her tightly. 'I called and called, but the poor dog never came . . . '

'Lara!' Desmond was pulling her back as she tried to make her way through the little garden she had kept so neat and tidy was now a disaster area of smouldering, water-drenched charcoal. 'Come on, Lara. Let me take you all back home with me. We'll work something out.'

'I'm not going without Spike,' she insisted and saw a flash of impatience as he continued to drag her away.

'What's so special about that damned dog?' he demanded roughly, pushing her towards the waiting car where her mother sat with worried eyes and parchment white features. 'At least you're all right and so are the children. And that's all that matters.'

How could she expect him to feel the same as she did? To him, Spike was nothing but a dirty, slobbering animal. Lara's heart constricted as she thought of the years of faithful companionship the old dog had given her.

Of course, the children were more important than anything in her life. That went without saying. But it didn't stop her loving that silly, dumb canine ragbag with all her heart.

★   ★   ★

No-one had seen Spike. Desmond had grown tetchy as she made him wait until she checked all the dog's favourite places and made sure that everyone would be keeping an eye open for him.

'He was old, Lara,' Evelyn said as they finally drove away from the scene of devastation. 'No doubt the fire was too much for him. He probably went off somewhere to die. They say they do that, you know.'

Lara nodded, sniffed loudly and scrubbed at the tears that were coursing down her cheeks. Tim and Janie cuddled into her, trying to comfort her. They loved Spike too, but right from the start, he had been Lara's dog.

'We could put a message out on internet,' Tim said.

'Like Dad did?' Janie showed some enthusiasm.

'No more internet,' Lara croaked and blew her nose, looking bleakly out of the car window, hoping to see old Spike lolloping along, pink tongue dangling, eyes bright with joy.

'Have we lost everything?' Tim wanted to know as if the gravity of their situation had only just hit him.

'Everything,' Lara said, thinking of the bricks and mortar that had cried out for attention, the windows that needed adjusting, floors and ceilings that needed replacing. Well, she no longer had to face the impossible task of renovating.

'We'll drop Evelyn off first,' Desmond said over his shoulder and Lara saw her mother smile contentedly at him. 'Thankfully, there's plenty of room at Sea View. Tomorrow, we'll talk about the future.'

Lara bit her lip, cuddled her children,

and tried to concentrate on the black, greasy tarmac of the road as it slipped by. It was better to have an empty head than worry about her losses. Or to think of a future that was far from sure in her mind or her heart.

14

She had half expected to find Martin still there, but Desmond explained that her 'ex' took off the minute Evelyn's call came in about the fire.

'I doubt he'll be back,' Desmond said, handing Lara a small glass of brandy. 'He's very good at running off in the face of adversity, isn't he?'

'That's not true!' It was Tim who spoke rather sharply, his earlier animosity forgotten.

'No, he's lovely,' added Janie, glancing for confirmation at her mother. 'He wouldn't go off and leave us. Not now.'

'No,' Tim added, then shuffled his feet. 'He wants to take us to France with him. He's got a big house and animals and lots of land and . . . '

'That's enough, you two,' Desmond bristled. 'Go on up to your rooms and I don't want to see you down here until breakfast tomorrow morning.'

Lara saw both twins wince. They weren't accustomed to being spoken to so severely. She was tempted to take Desmond to task on the issue, but suddenly she was too exhausted to do anything but just sit there and be looked after, even if it was Desmond doing it.

'Do as you're told,' she told the children gently and gave a reassuring smile when they turned appealing eyes on her. 'We're all far too tired to argue.'

They went without a murmur, not even dragging their feet and she knew that they were in as great a shock as she was. She would go up to them later and they could all huddle on one of the beds and comfort one another.

It seemed that the only comfort they would get from Desmond, was cold comfort. But then, she was overwrought and she ought to be more grateful to him, ought to think more kindly of him.

'I'm sorry to involve you in my troubles,' she said, having found him staring at her contemplatively. 'It's really very kind of you . . . '

'Kindness has nothing to do with it, Lara,' he cut her off quickly and paced the room. 'Look, when I thought you were still in love with Martin, I stepped out of the picture, but I now take it that you won't be getting back together after all?'

'No, I don't think that's possible. Not any more.' Lara's throat constricted and she averted her gaze as tears of sadness welled up in them.

'It's true that we hardly know one another,' Desmond continued, 'but I think we could make a go of it. It's sooner than I anticipated, but given the circumstances — will you marry me?'

Lara gave a gasp. Her mouth opened and closed, she blinked up at him and took a gulp of her brandy, which made her cough, but she was thankful for the warm courage it sent coursing through her veins.

'As you say, Desmond, it's much too soon, but . . . '

They both jumped as the doorbell trilled out loudly. Desmond's face twisted with displeasure and she heard a subdued oath as he went to answer the summons. When he came back, he looked even more disgruntled. Lara saw, with a leap of her heart, that he was not alone.

'Martin!'

Martin looked dishevelled and there were black smears over his face. In his arms he carried a grey, furry bundle with mournful eyes that emitted a mournful whimper, then yelped with pleasure on seeing Lara.

'Spike! Oh, you found him!'

The reunion with Spike was a tearful one. At the sound of the dog's elated barking, the children came rushing back into the room and there were hugs and kisses all round.

'I was with Desmond when Evelyn phoned. I drove over to see if I could help, but I was too late.' Martin stared directly into Lara's eyes and a quiver set her whole body alive. 'When I heard that you had come back here, but that Spike here was missing, I knew I couldn't come back without him.'

'Oh, thank you, Martin — thank you so much!' Lara leaned forward and placed her lips on his cheek and felt his fingers tighten around her arm.

'You see, Desmond,' Tim shouted out, his face bright and rosy with pleasure. 'You were wrong. My dad did come back. He's not going to leave us again, ever.'

He transferred his gaze to his father's face and Martin stroked the boy's head. It was the gesture of a man filled with love. She had never seen Desmond do that, even to his own children. He had never been separated from them, and yet there seemed to be little if any affection.

'I suppose this little gallant act of yours is designed to knock me out of the running.' Desmond was addressing Martin, but his eyes slid over to Lara to see her response. 'It happens that I've just proposed marriage.'

'Oh? Is that true, Lara?'

Martin's eyes became dark with anxiety. He took up both her hands and held them close to his heart. She could feel the beat of his life force and felt drawn in like a piece of metal to a large magnet.

The magic that had existed between them so long ago had not died. She had never stopped loving him.

Desmond wanted her, she was almost sure, as a dutiful wife and mother to their children. But it took more than that to make a marriage.

'Yes, Martin, it is true,' she said with a slightly lopsided smile. 'But you arrived just as I was about to give him my answer.'

'Which is?' His hands tightened on hers as he drew her closer until they might well be one being in the same familiar skin.

Lara glanced across at Desmond, who already looked resigned to the situation.

'I'm sorry, Desmond,' she said softly.

'I can't possible marry you. You see, I'm already married — to the only man I have ever loved. And I've never stopped loving him — or waiting for him to come back into my life.'

The twins broke out into an ecstatic chorus of words and questions and everything rolled into one as Spike joined in with a mighty howl.

'Do they allow English dogs into France?' she asked and Martin laughed as he took her face between his hands and kissed her firmly on the lips.

'Yes, well, I'll leave you to it, then,' Desmond said resignedly.

His words went unnoticed as he ushered his own two children out of the room and went with them, quietly closing the door behind him.

THE END

We do hope that you have enjoyed reading this large print book.

Did you know that all of our titles are available for purchase?

We publish a wide range of high quality large print books including:
Romances, Mysteries, Classics
General Fiction
Non Fiction and Westerns

Special interest titles available in large print are:
The Little Oxford Dictionary
Music Book, Song Book
Hymn Book, Service Book

Also available from us courtesy of Oxford University Press:
Young Readers' Dictionary
(large print edition)
Young Readers' Thesaurus
(large print edition)

For further information or a free brochure, please contact us at:
Ulverscroft Large Print Books Ltd.,
The Green, Bradgate Road, Anstey,
Leicester, LE7 7FU, England.
Tel: (00 44) **0116 236 4325**
Fax: (00 44) **0116 234 0205**

Other titles in the
Linford Romance Library:

THE EAGLE STONE

Heather Pardoe

While assisting her father in selling provisions to visitors to the top of Snowdon, Elinor Owen meets the adventuress Lady Sara Raglan and her handsome nephew, Richard. Eli is swiftly drawn into Lady Sara's most recent adventure, becoming a spy for Queen Victoria's government. Now, up against the evil Jacques, Eli and Richard are soon fighting for their lives, while Lady Sara heads for a final showdown and pistols at dawn with Jacques on the summit of Snowdon itself.

THE ~~~~ PIER

E
L
T
w
"
l
C
sl
w
a
tl
o
h